Mouse Guard

Alphabet

Book

Published by
ARCHAIA™

For the youngfurs just learning their letters,
the oldfurs who want to teach them,
and every other mouse in between.

Mouse Guard.
Alphabet
Book

Written by
David Petersen

Illustrated by
Serena Malyon

COVER BY **SERENA MALYON**

DESIGNER **KARA LEOPARD**
ASSOCIATE EDITOR **CAMERON CHITTOCK**
EDITOR **BRYCE CARLSON**

ROSS RICHIE CEO & Founder
MATT GAGNON Editor-in-Chief
FILIP SABLIK President of Publishing & Marketing
STEPHEN CHRISTY President of Development
LANCE KREITER VP of Licensing & Merchandising
PHIL BARBARO VP of Finance
ARUNE SINGH VP of Marketing
BRYCE CARLSON Managing Editor
MEL CAYLO Marketing Manager
SCOTT NEWMAN Production Design Manager
KATE HENNING Operations Manager
SIERRA HAHN Senior Editor
DAFNA PLEBAN Editor, Talent Development
SHANNON WATTERS Editor
ERIC HARBURN Editor
WHITNEY LEOPARD Editor
JASMINE AMIRI Editor

CHRIS ROSA Associate Editor
ALEX GALER Associate Editor
CAMERON CHITTOCK Associate Editor
MATTHEW LEVINE Assistant Editor
SOPHIE PHILIPS-ROBERTS Assistant Editor
KELSEY DIETERICH Designer
JILLIAN CRAB Production Designer
MICHELLE ANKLEY Production Designer
KARA LEOPARD Production Designer
GRACE PARK Production Designer Assistant
ELIZABETH LOUGHRIDGE Accounting Coordinator
STEPHANIE HOCUTT Social Media Coordinator
JOSÉ MEZA Event Coordinator
JAMES ARRIOLA Mailroom Assistant
HOLLY AITCHISON Operations Assistant
MEGAN CHRISTOPHER Operations Assistant
AMBER PARKER Administrative Assistant

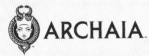

MOUSE GUARD ALPHABET BOOK, September 2017.
Published by Archaia, a division of Boom Entertainment,
Inc. Mouse Guard is ™ & © 2017 David Petersen. All Rights
Reserved. Archaia™ and the Archaia logo are trademarks of
Boom Entertainment, Inc., registered in various countries and
categories. All characters, events, and institutions depicted herein are fictional. Any similarity between any of
the names, characters, persons, events, and/or institutions in this publication to actual names, characters, and
persons, whether living or dead, events, and/or institutions is unintended and purely coincidental.

BOOM! Studios, 5670 Wilshire Boulevard, Suite 450, Los Angeles, CA 90036-5679.
Printed in China. First Printing.

ISBN: 978-1-68415-010-6 , eISBN: 978-1-61398-681-3

is for
Apiary Keeper

With smoke to soothe the sting of a hive,
one mouse tames Lockhaven's bees.
With wax and honey Guardmice can thrive,
as the flying buzzers pollinate the trees.

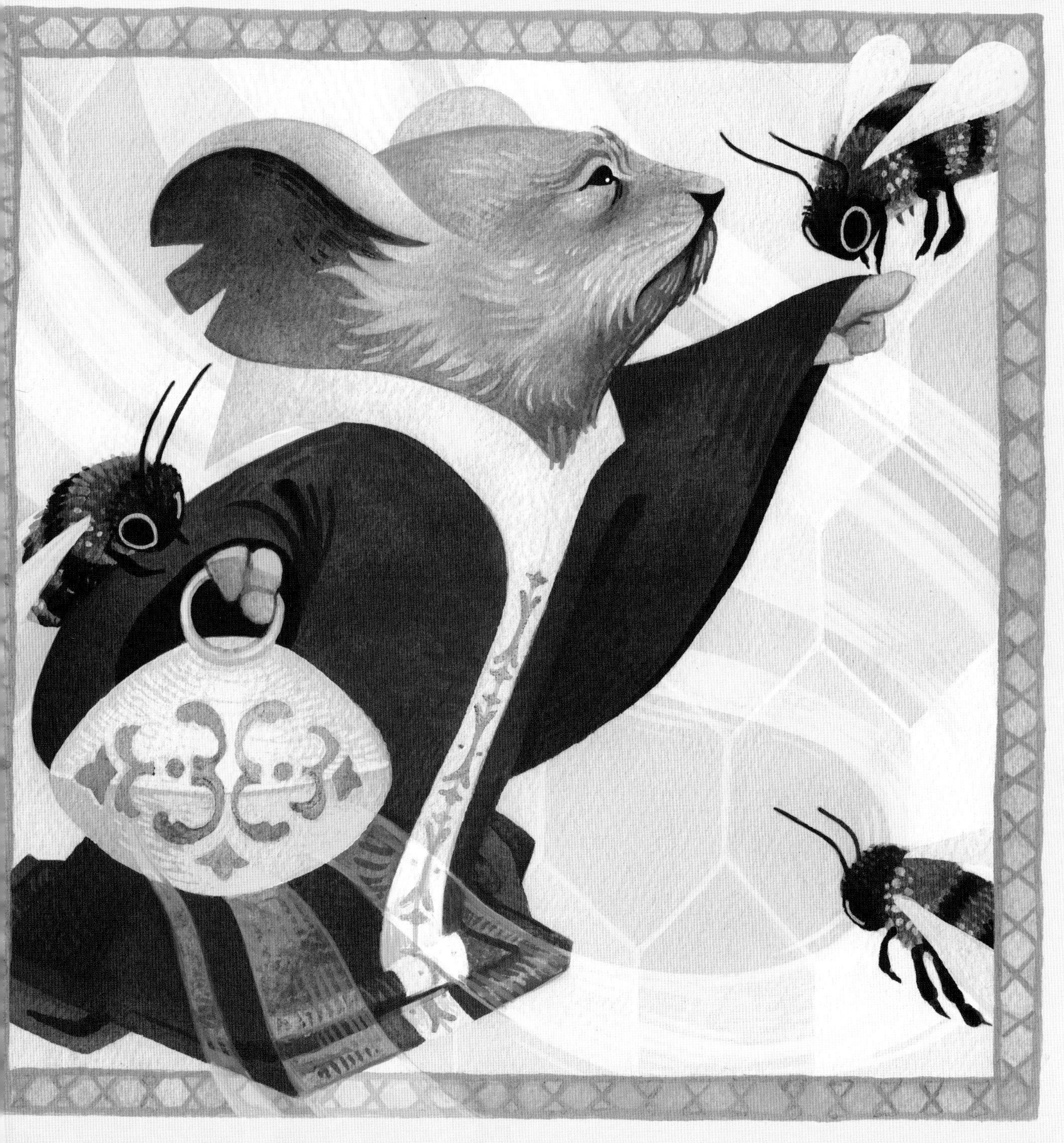

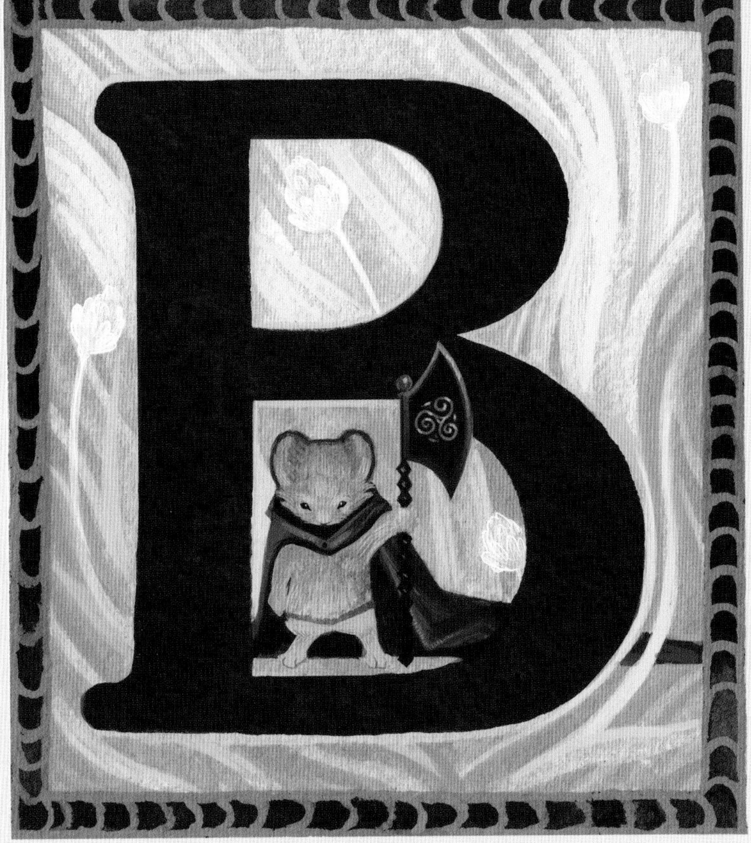
B

is for

Black Axe

Mouse with axe of black and legend of fable,
slay the snake, wolf, fox, and hawk.
You may hail anymouse willing and able,
a mouse of myth guards the haven of lock.

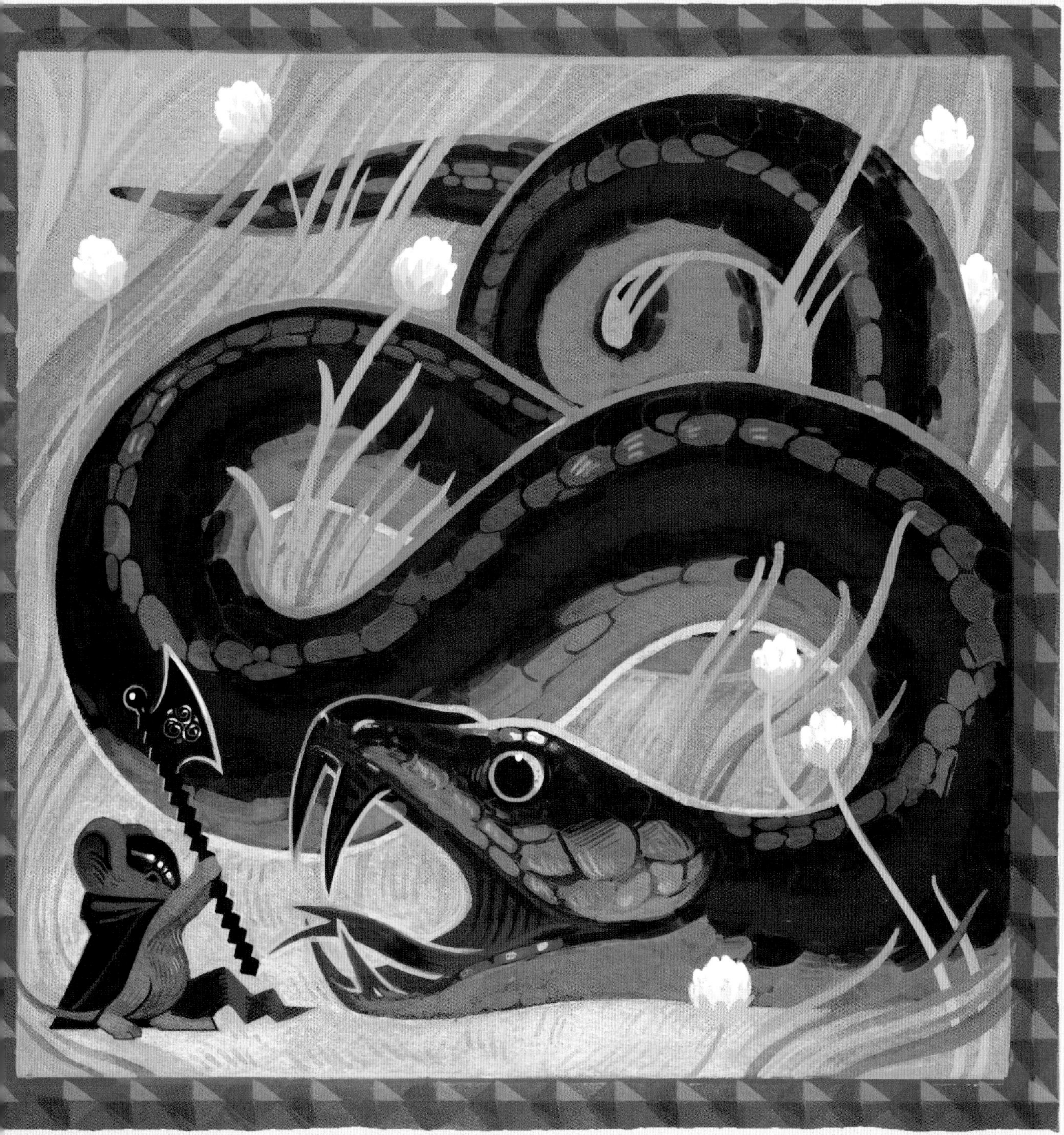

is for
Carpenter

By mallet and chisel, plane and saw,
mouse can shape the very nature of wood.
With skill and labor and steady trained paw,
things crafted where only timber once stood.

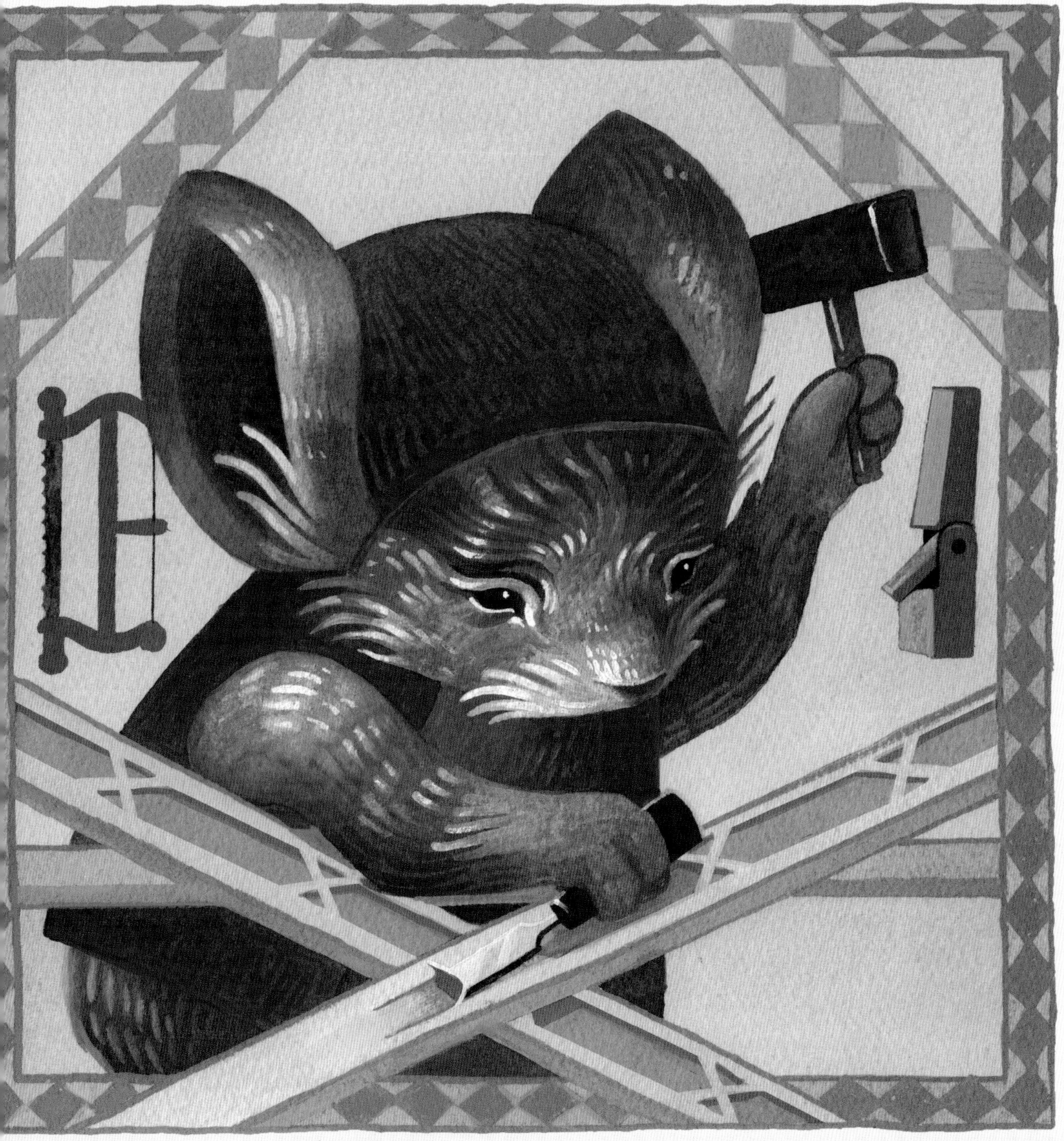

is for
Darkheather

Deep below our mousey lands above,
the kin of weasels sneak and hide.
Within a tiled den devoid of love,
mazes of tunnels lead far and wide.

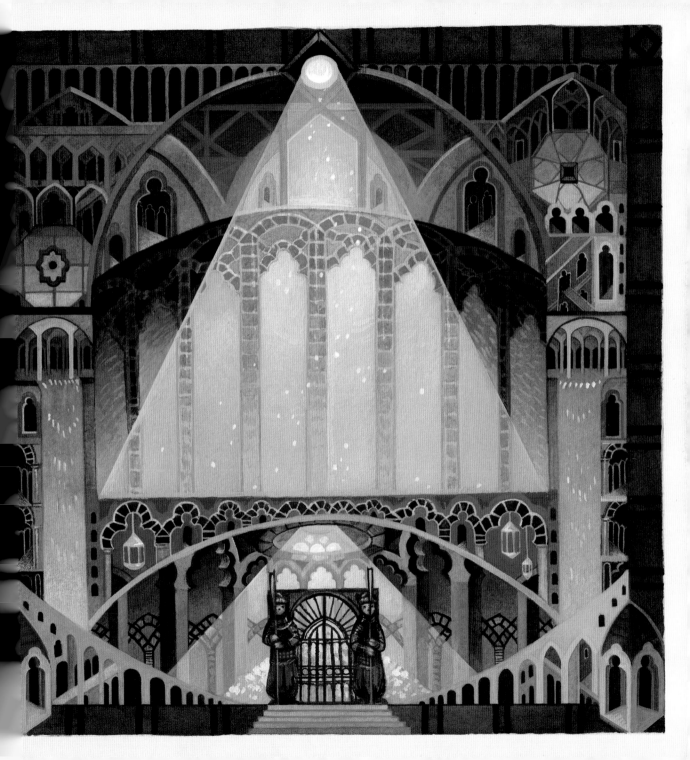

is for
Ebon Kingdom

North of the sea beyond most maps are wise,
lies a string of islands ruled by a ferret king.
A foe by nature but his fairness a surprise,
with deeds shared across seas on crow wing.

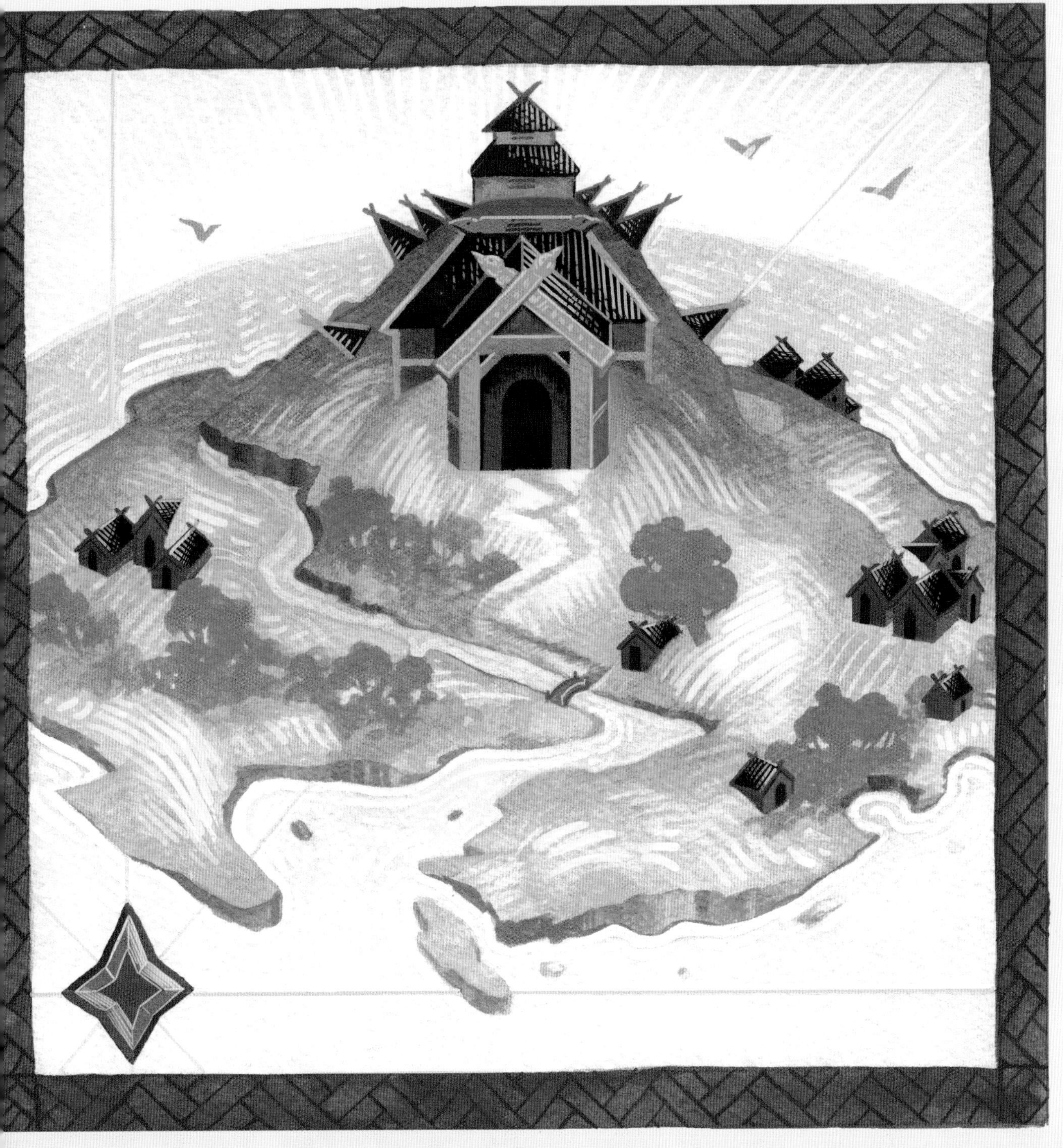

is for
Fox

Cunning tricks aid this sly redfurred foe,
goodmice decide to hide or take up spear.
On sunlit fields or freezing sheets of snow,
if a fox is loose a whole city lives in fear.

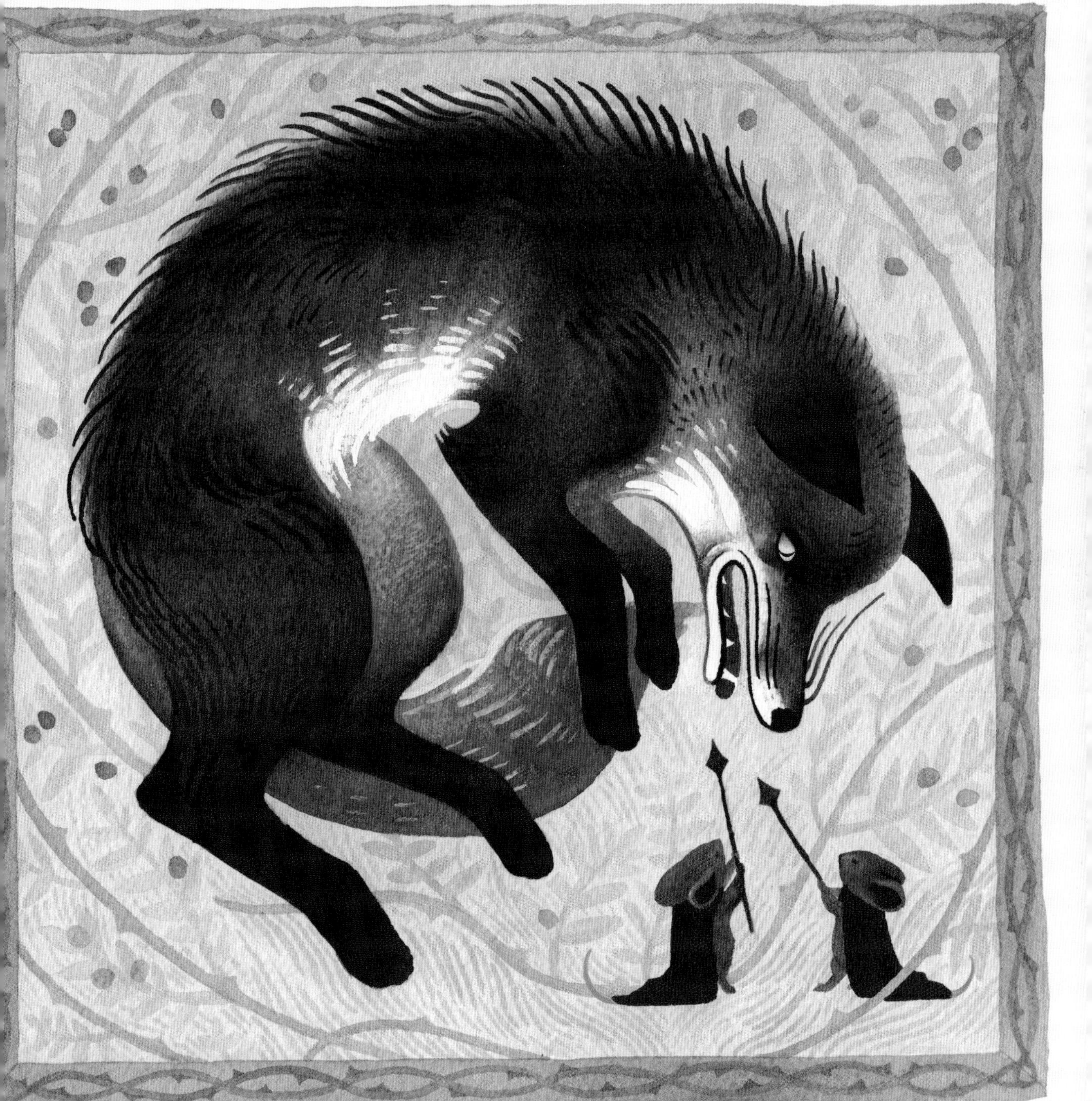

is for
Guardmouse

It takes more than a mouse of bladed deed,
in order for our kind to live and survive.
With service in heart and care in the lead,
a territory of mice will prevail and thrive.

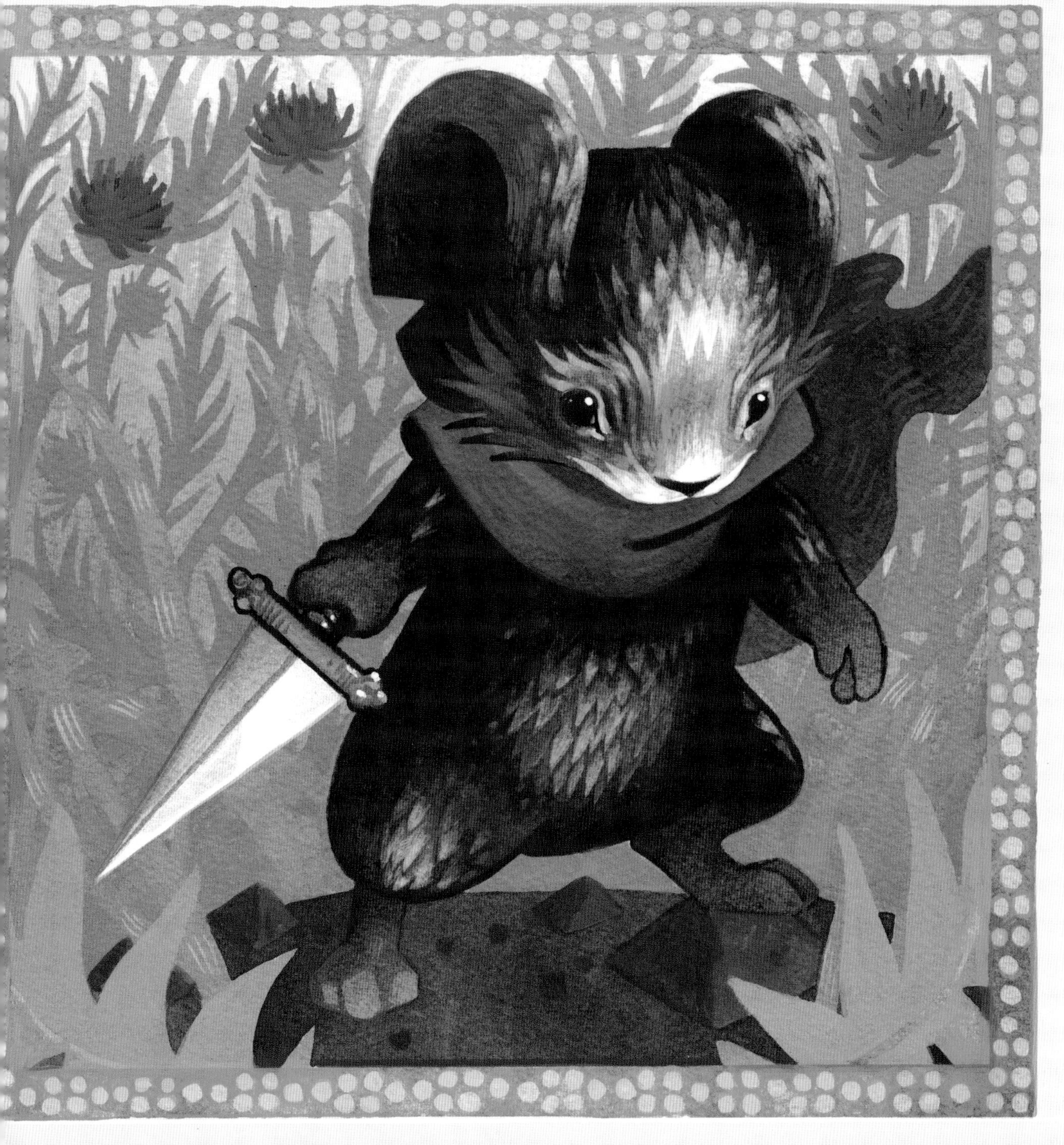

is for
Healer

For injured mice who are sick and ache,
those trained to heal use plants they know.
They make a rub, a wrap, an elixir to take,
well ever-after into old age they'll grow.

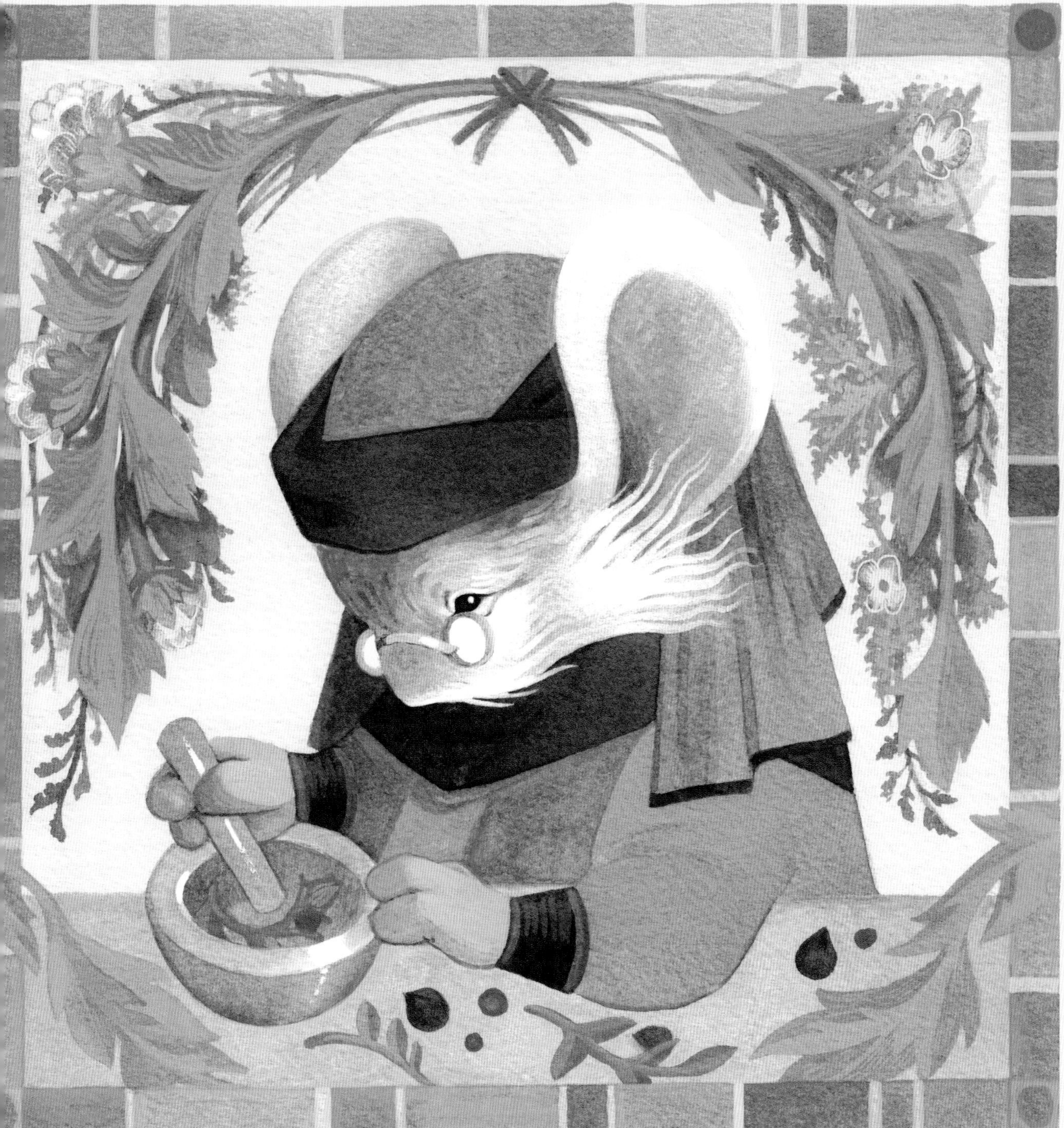

is for
Insectrist

Mice caretakers of moth, beetle, and cricket,
raise their own swarm, flock, and herd.
Clicking and chirping from bramble to thicket,
companions and laborers for we who are furred.

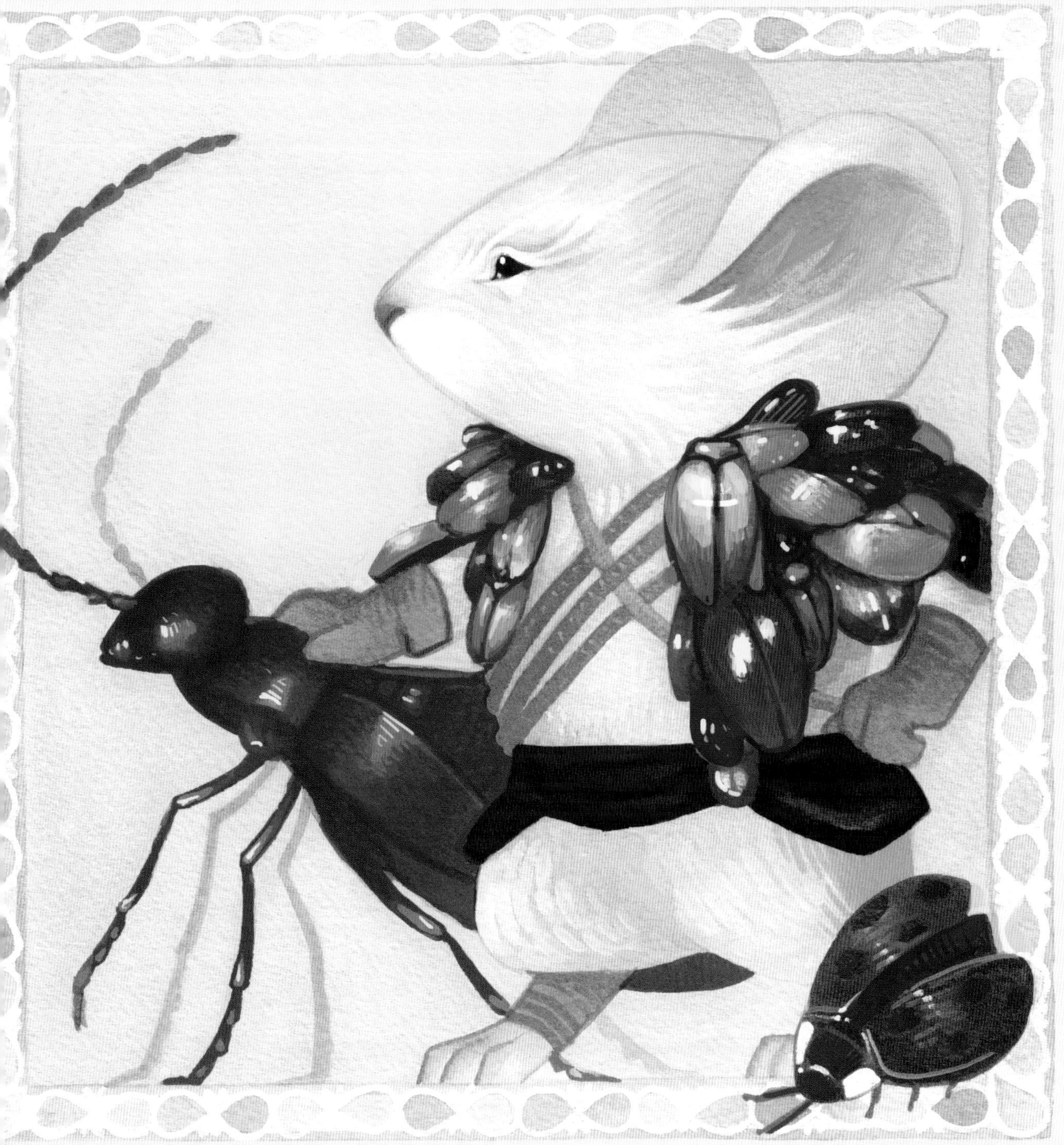

is for
June Alley Inn

Barkstone's famous merry tavern of tales,
where the hostess offers many a room for the night.
With the warmest of stews and coldest of ales,
a game and a legend will set anymouse right.

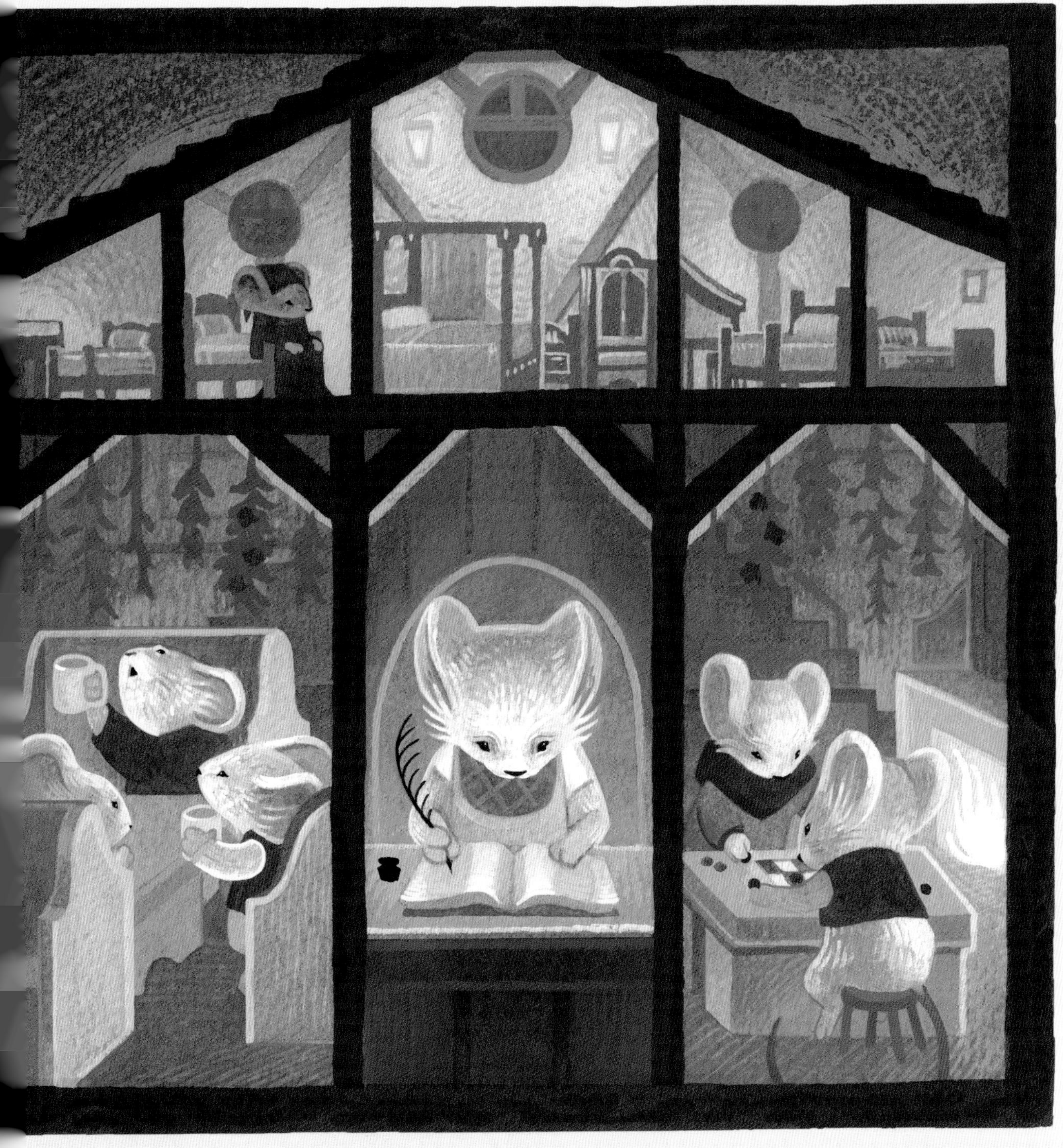

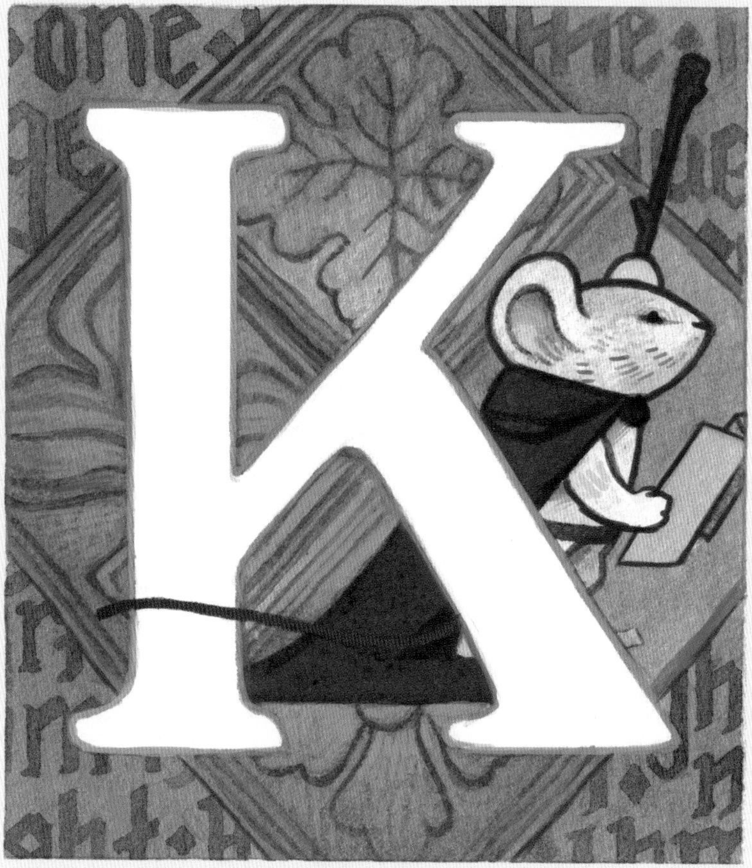
K

is for
Kenzie

The greyfur leader whose name means wise,
has ideas more powerful than any known blade.
He uses knowledge well wielded for mice to arise,
from a routine patrol or shifty weasel raid.

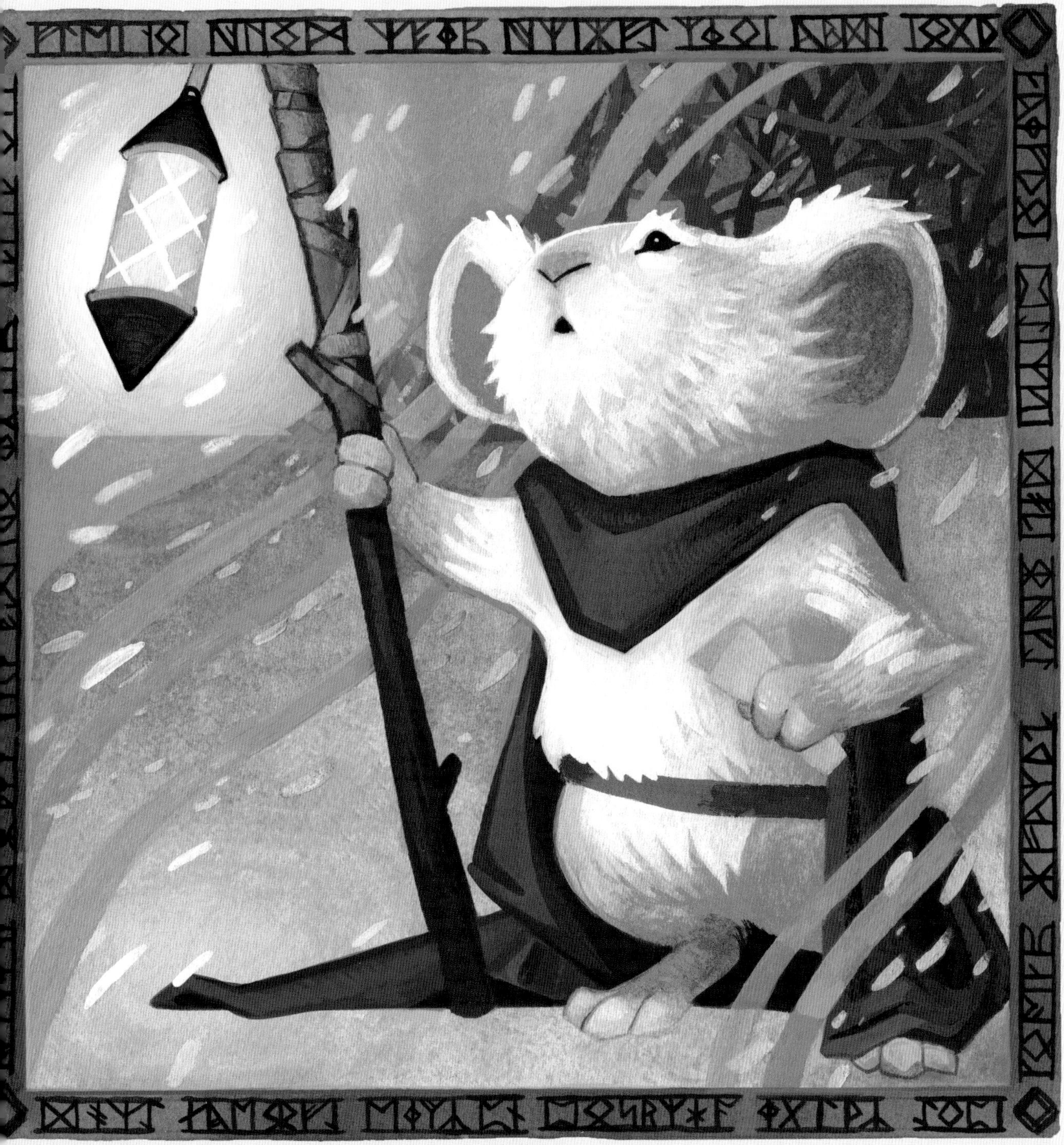

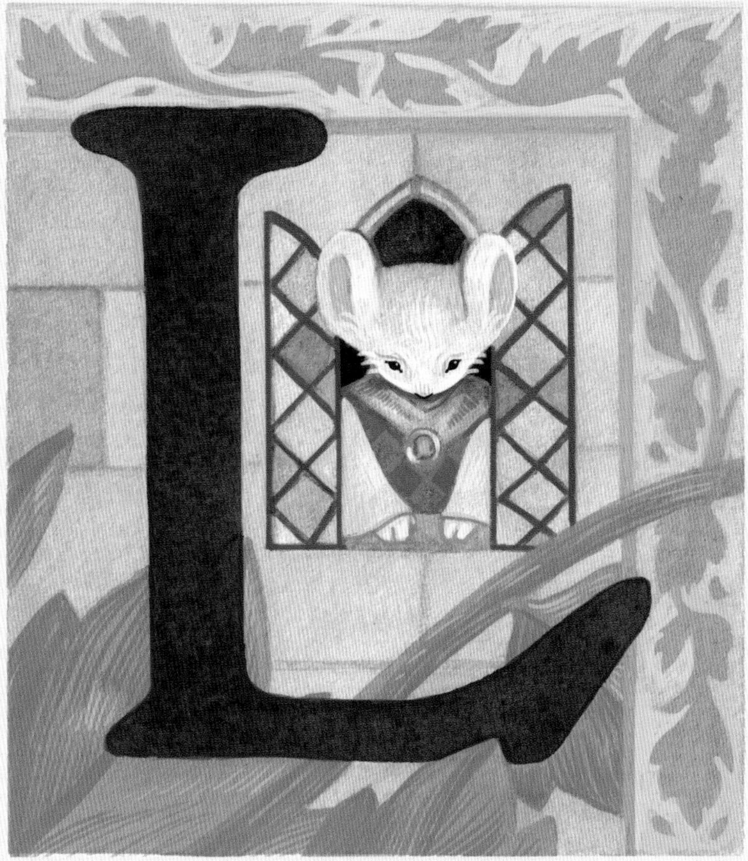
L

is for

Lockhaven

The castle of the Guard, for wherever they roam,
a beacon that stands for protection and charity.
More, it is a guard's conviction, pride, and home,
for the safety of all mice is a true rarity.

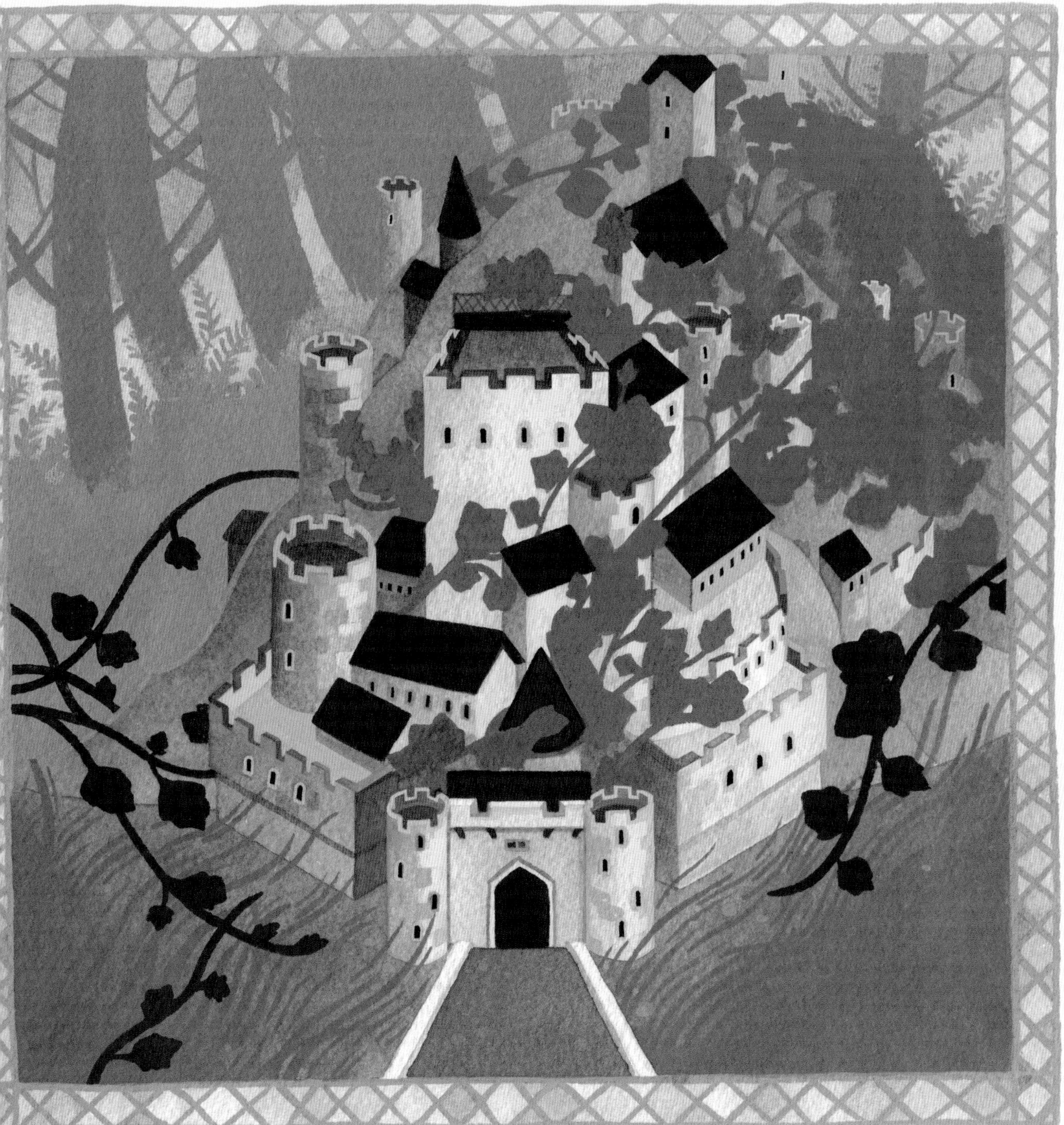

is for
Matriarch

From the start of the Guard a lady has reigned,
she commands but more importantly she leads.
To take up their task her Guardmice are trained:
deliver the service each common mouse needs.

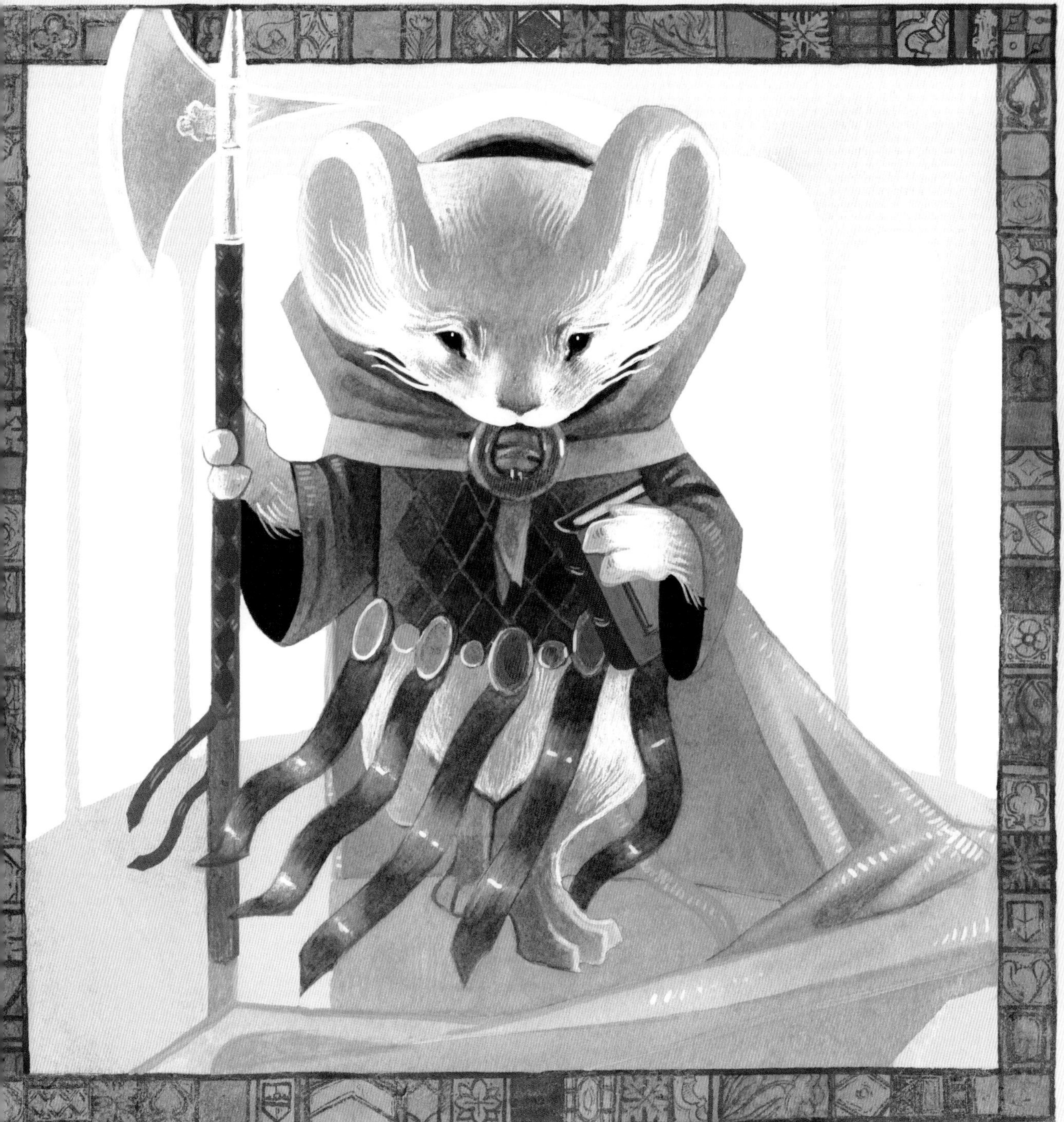

is for
Nature

We respect our land, our sea, our sky,
and every species living in between.
The fish swim, plants grow, and birds fly,
our wild world is a beautiful scene.

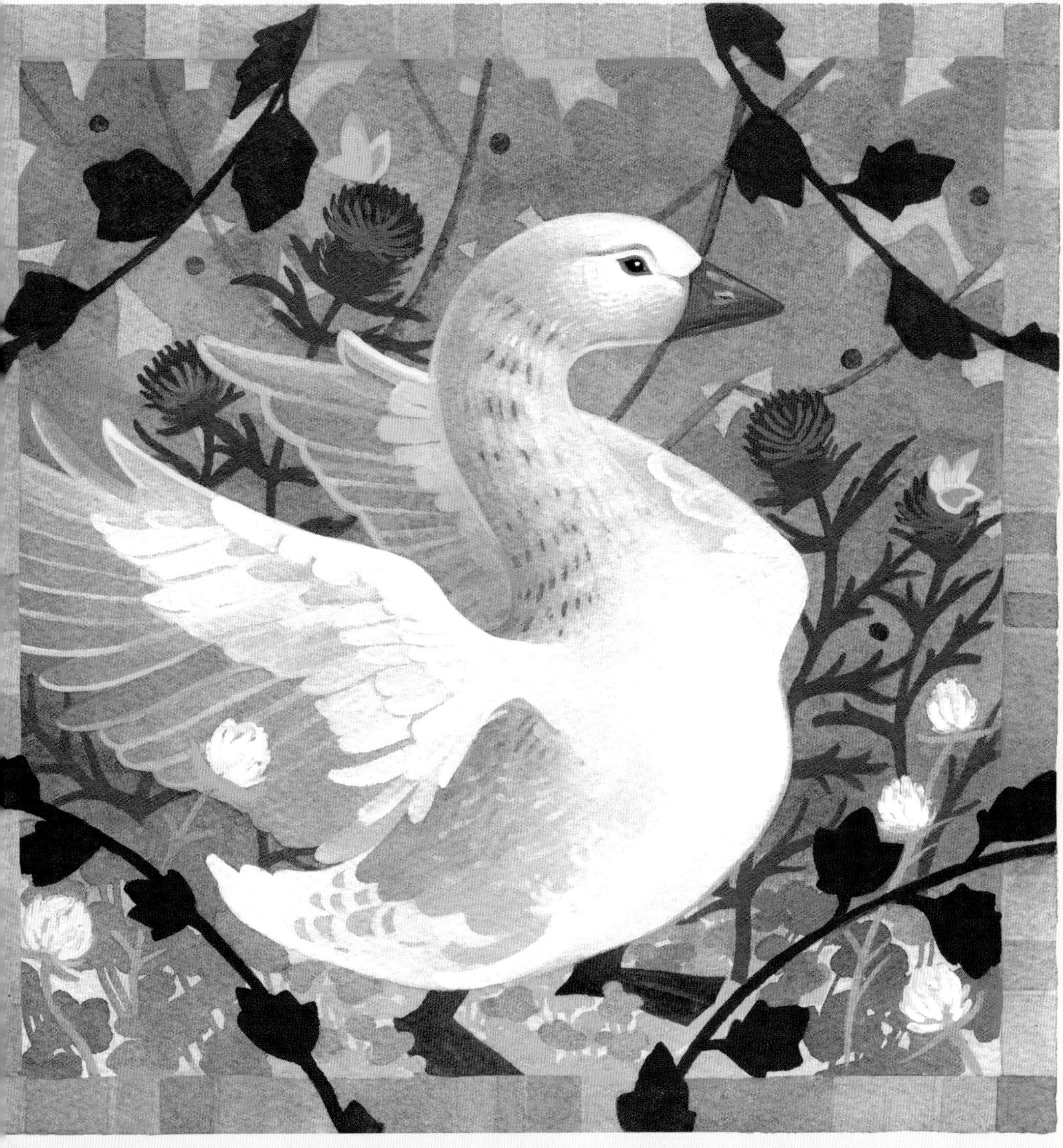

is for
Owl

Feathered hunters hoot out their call,
to moon and stars in the darkness of night.
On silent wings they hunt the small,
when evening comes, beware their flight.

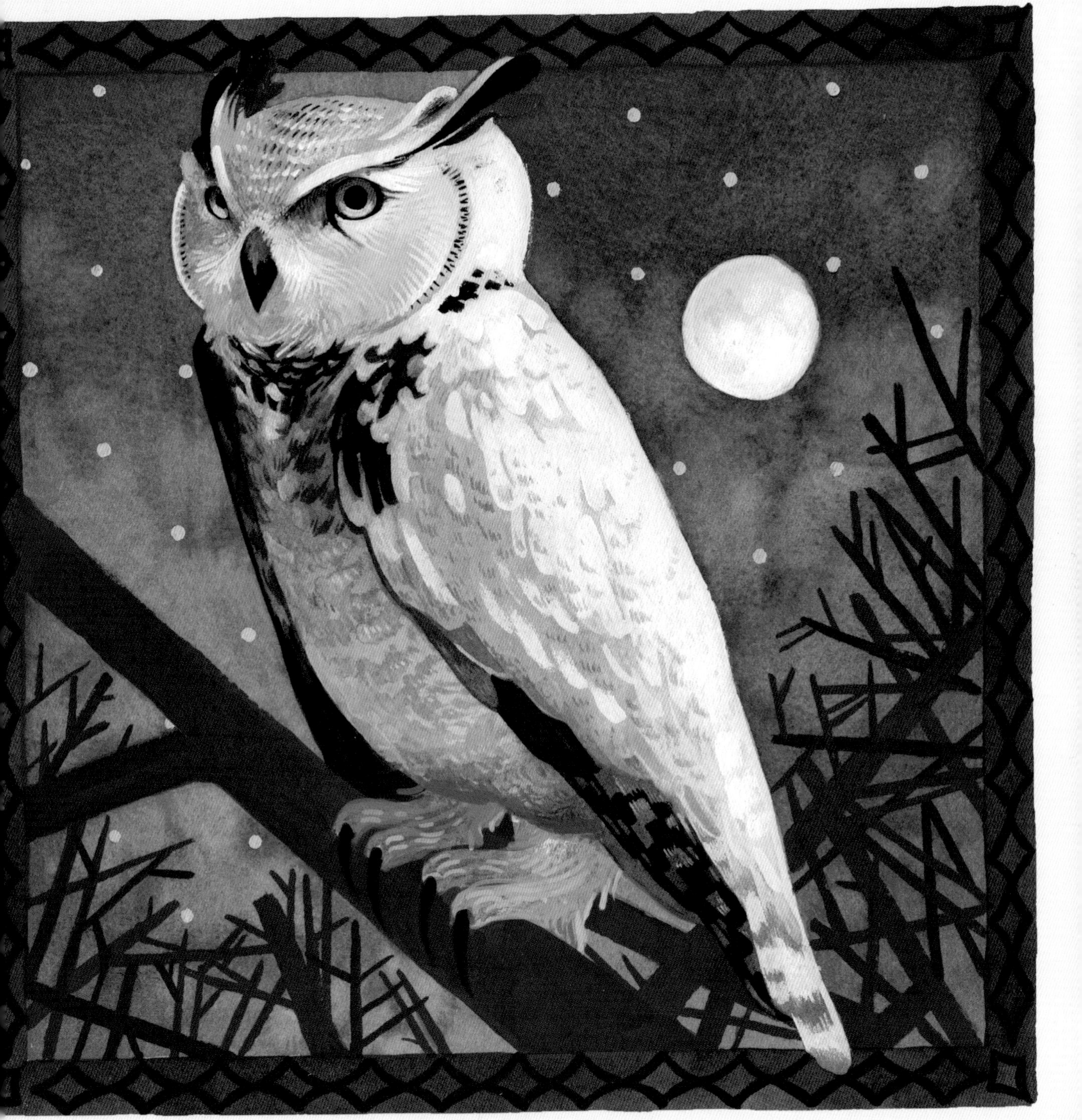

is for
Potter

The mouse skilled to handle clay in their paws,
will make you the finest pitcher, pot, or platter.
It goes into the kiln to be baked without flaws,
for the crafts that we use are the ones that most matter.

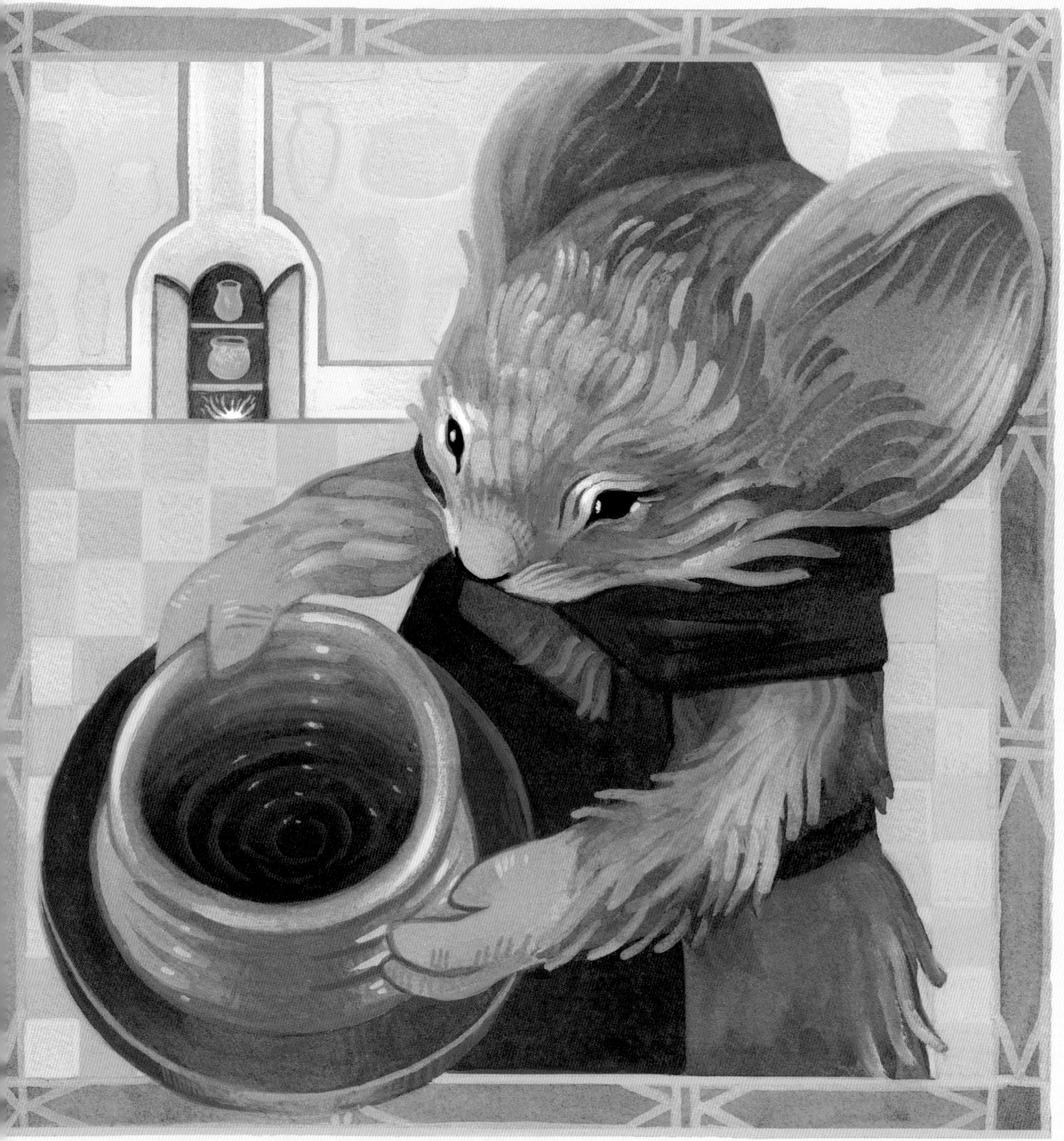

is for
Quiet

Goodmice are careful to always keep silent,
out in the wild where dangerous beasts stray.
They can be scary, and terrible, and violent,
so lie very still until they're well on their way.

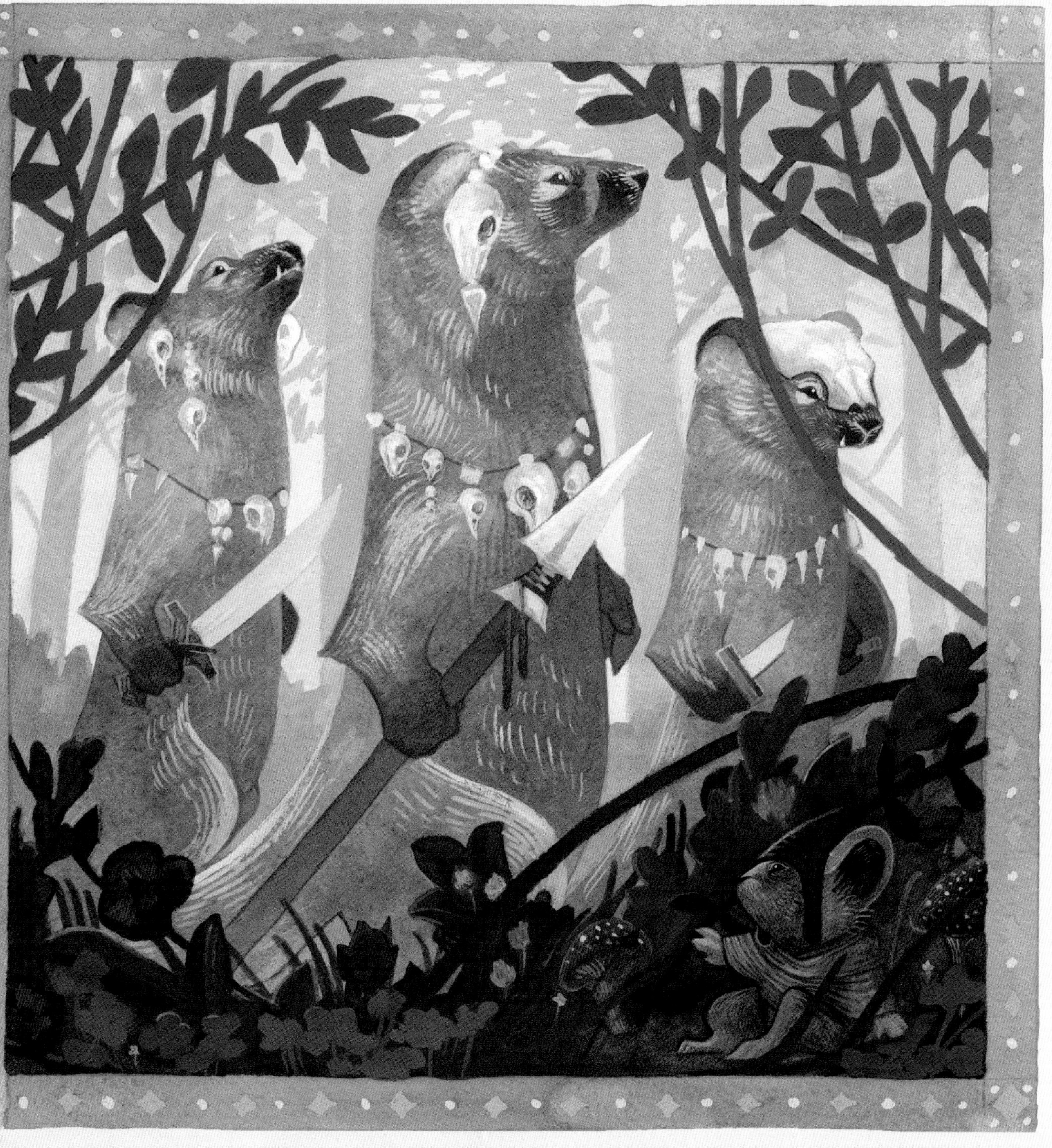

is for
Rand

The protector of mice whose name means shield,
he stands in the way of a predator's blows.
Defending mousekind in wild forest or field,
no matter the danger or attack a beast throws.

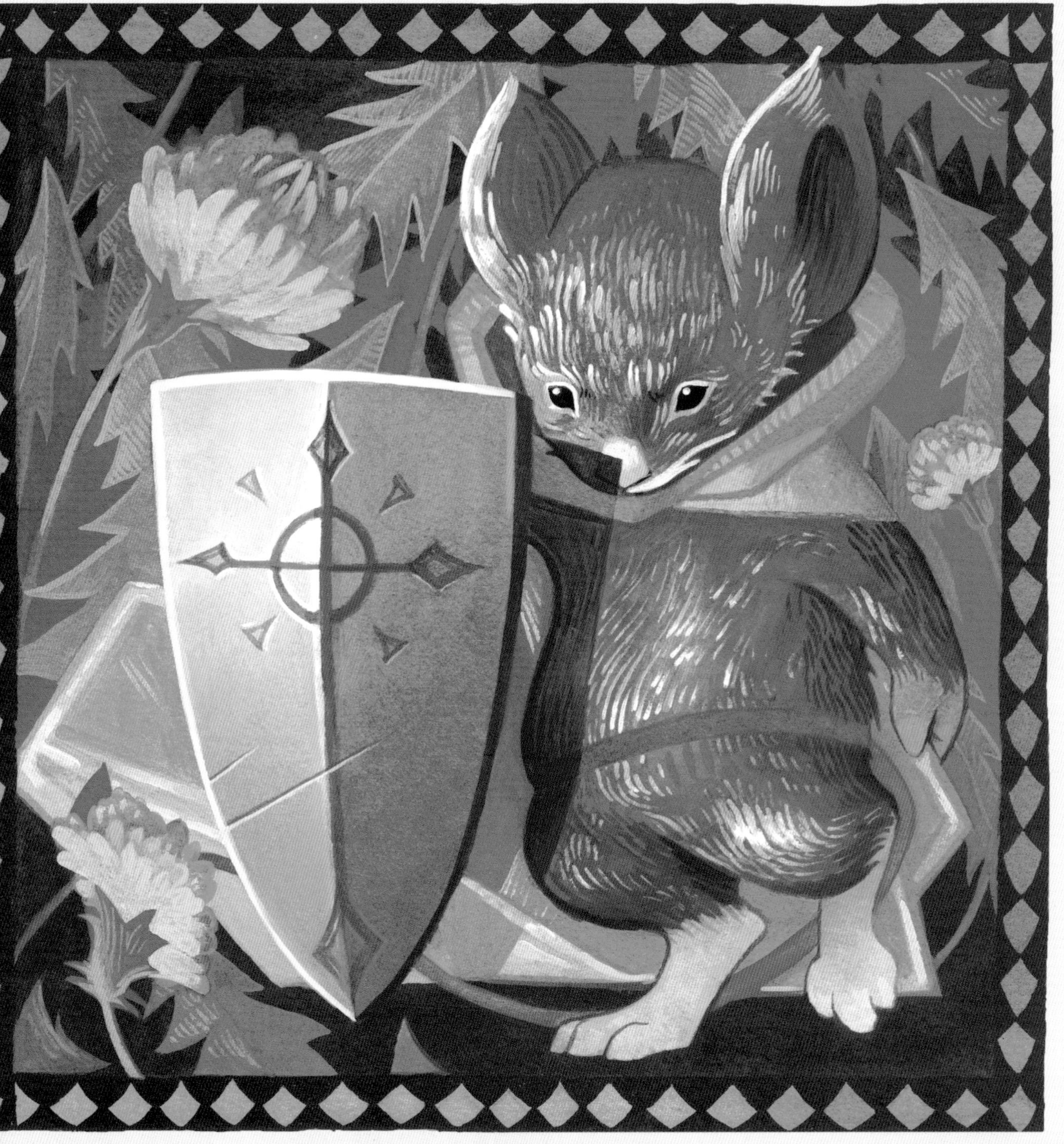

is for
Saxon

The brave mouse whose name means sword,
leaps quickly to action with no pause or delay.
In frightful times it's danger he moves toward,
his heart and his deeds are the Guard on display.

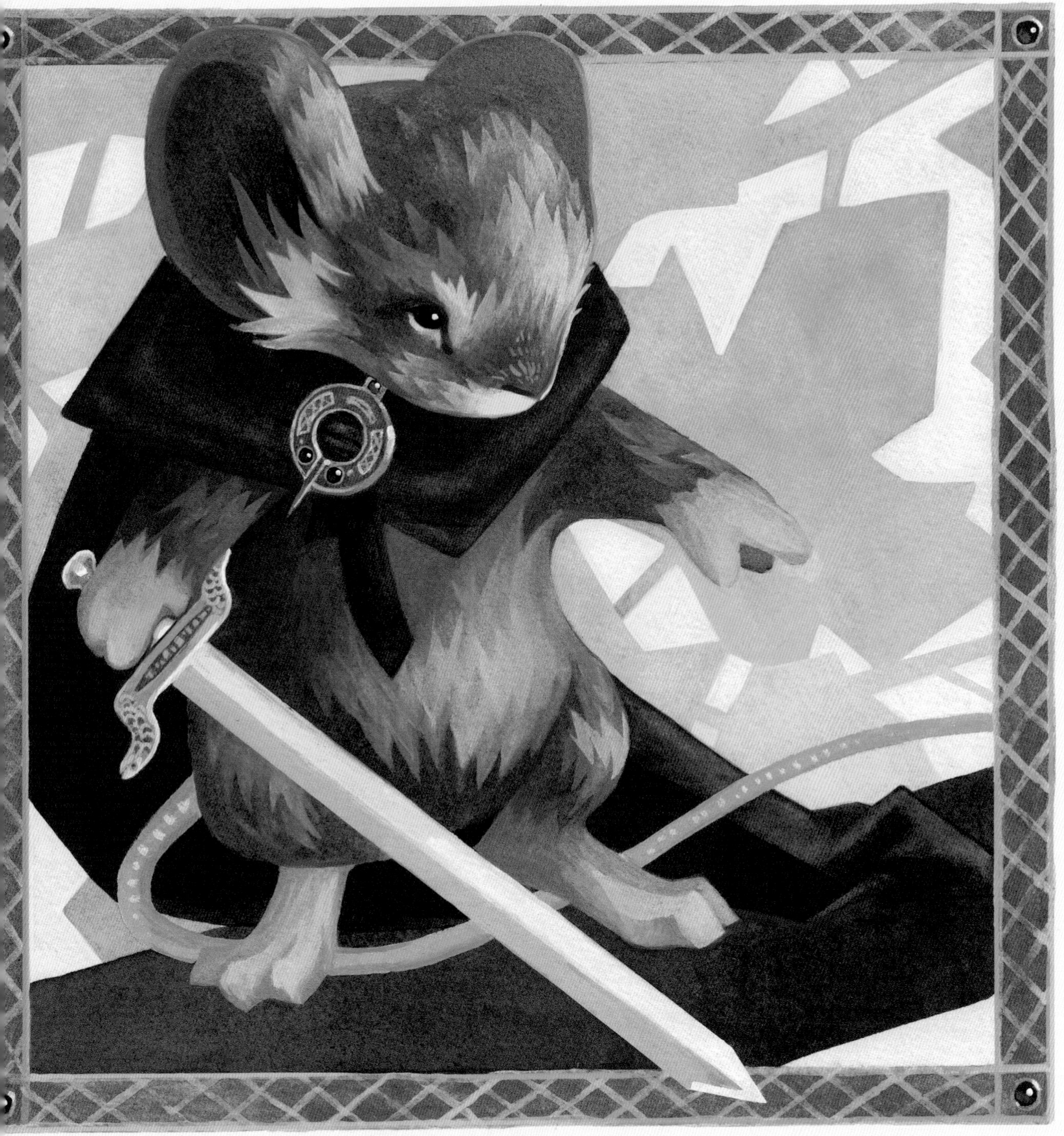

is for
Toad

Hear the croak song of the lilypad sitters,
in the tall soggy reeds as dragonflies swarm.
Warts and all their chorus warbles and jitters,
the pitch of their voice may warn of a storm.

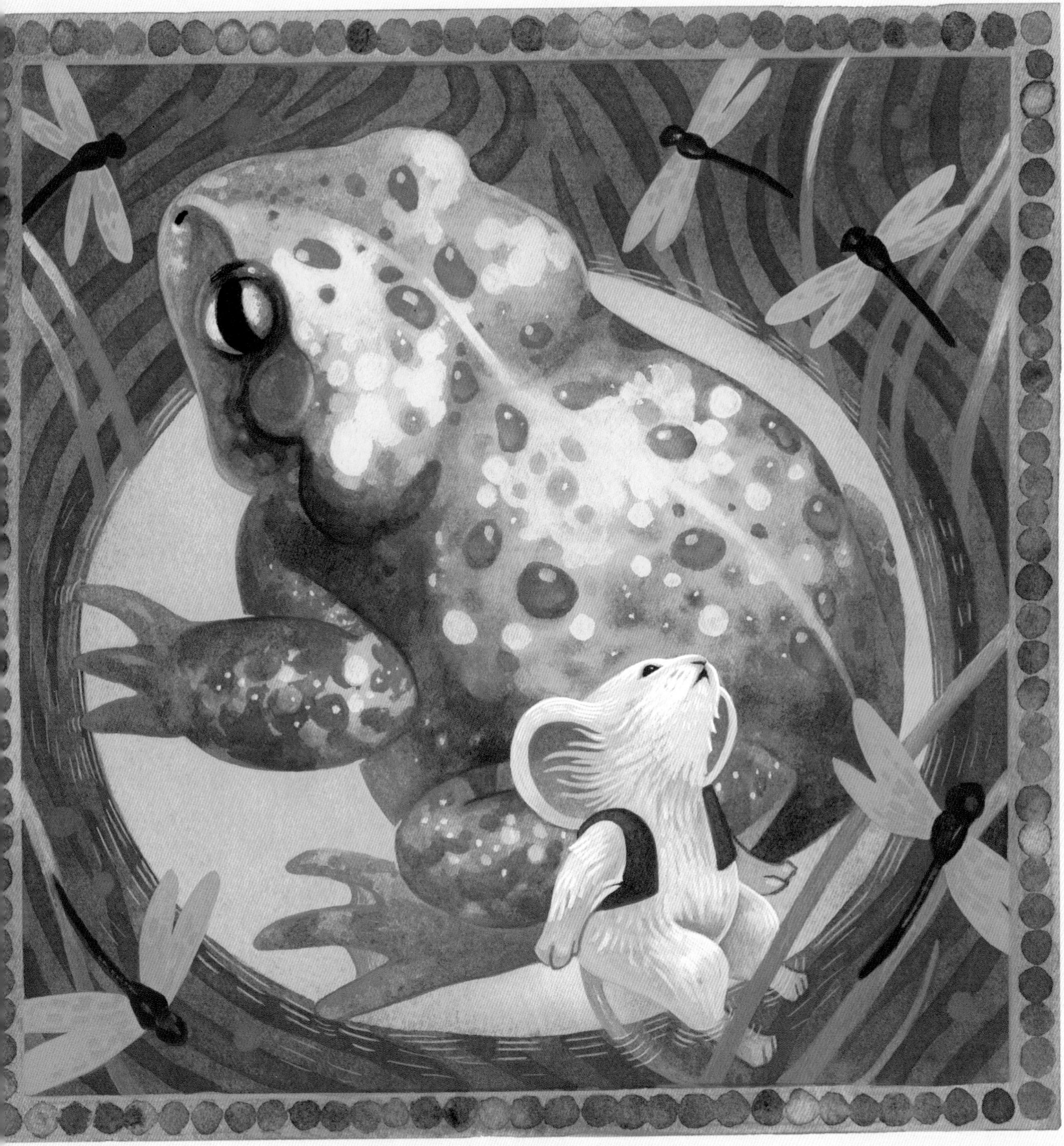

is for
Unity

Working together makes little mice strong,
with love of liberty, the Guard gather to survive.
Beasts of the air, land, and sky hear our song,
we shall do more than just live, united we thrive.

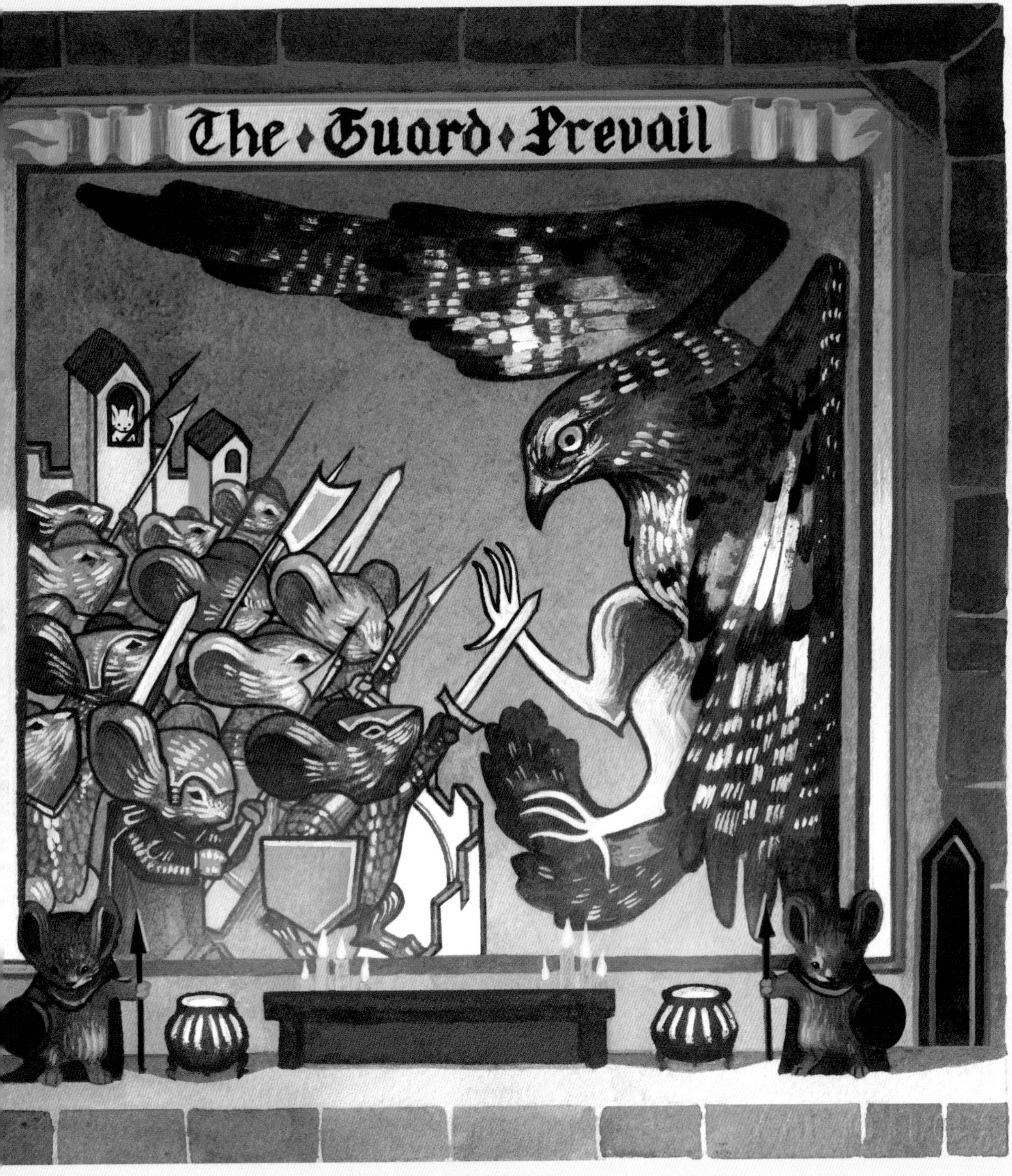
The • Guard • Prevail

is for
Vernalstar

Spring arrives when the south star appears,
the colorful season when plants bud and flower.
Dance and make merry, sing and shout cheers,
parade while you can before rains start to shower.

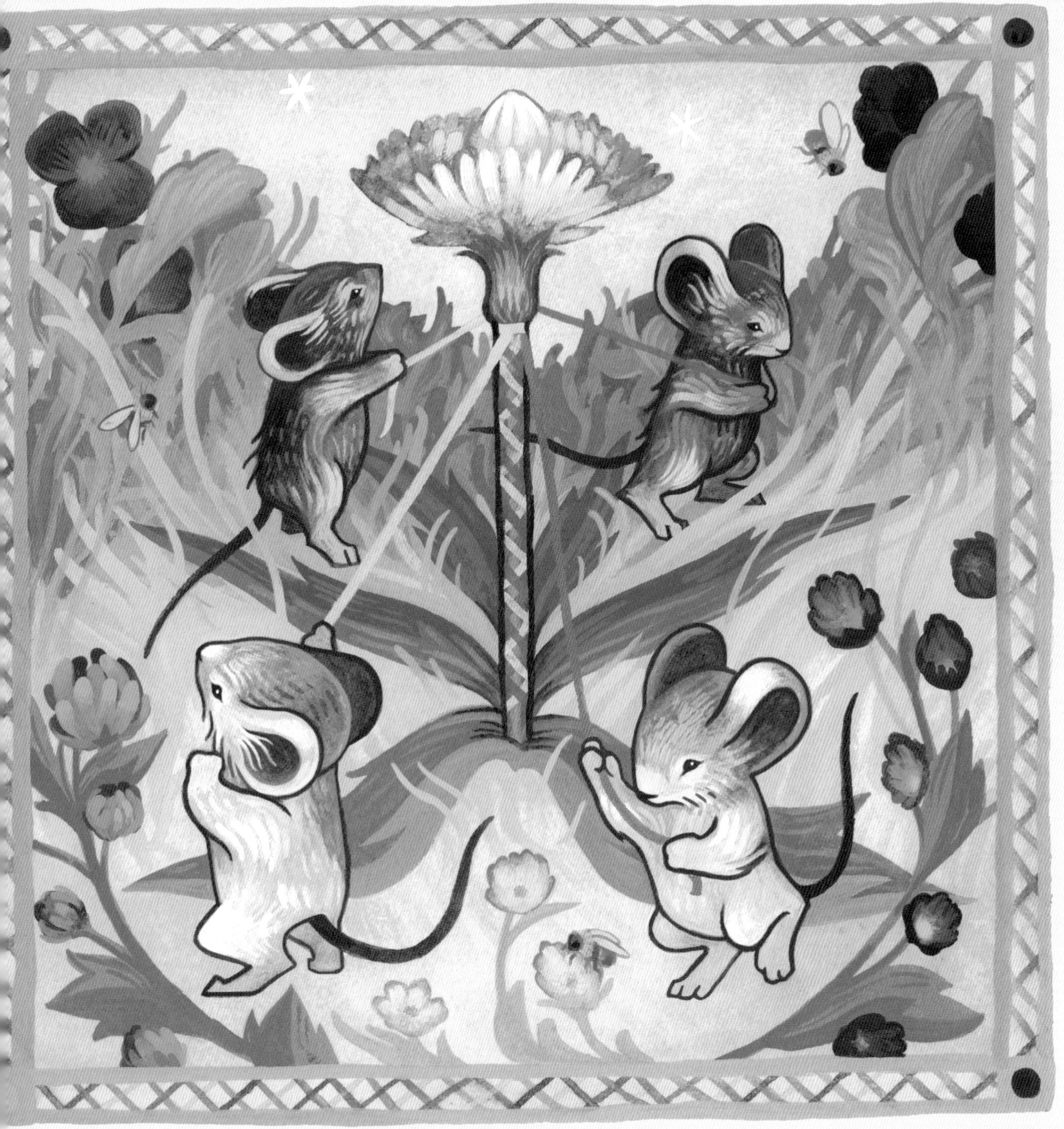

is for
Weather Watcher

Mice who study when changing winds blow,
find signals in crickets, leaves, and soil.
Be it frost, gale, rain, or heat they'll still know,
to prepare us for weather and never for spoil.

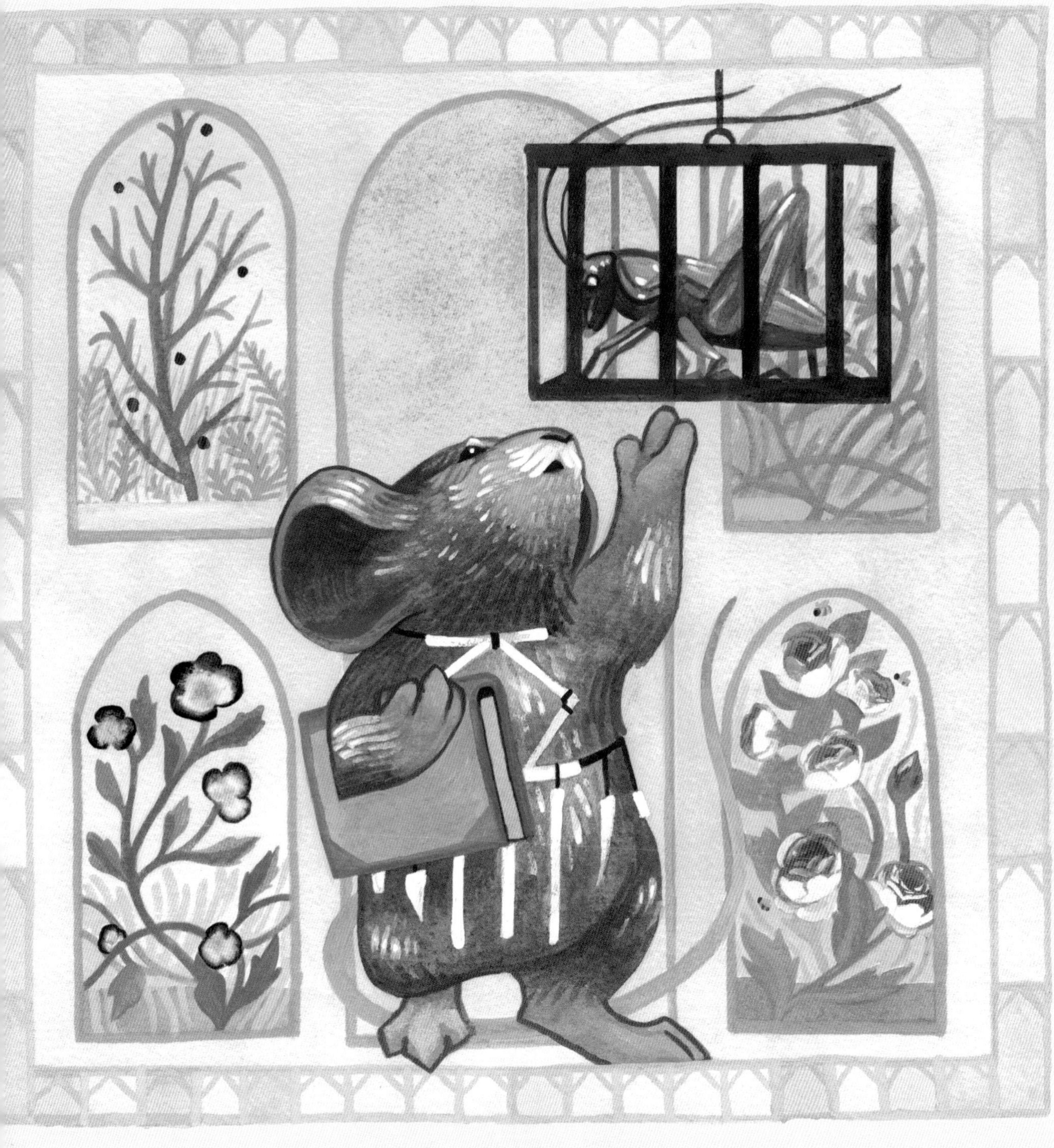

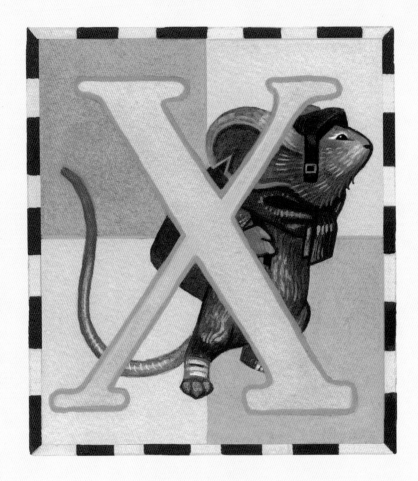

Marks the Spot

When mapping a route crisscross a mark,
for that is the spot your patrol should arrive.
Through fields and streams, daylight and dark,
it's the path that's important to get there alive.

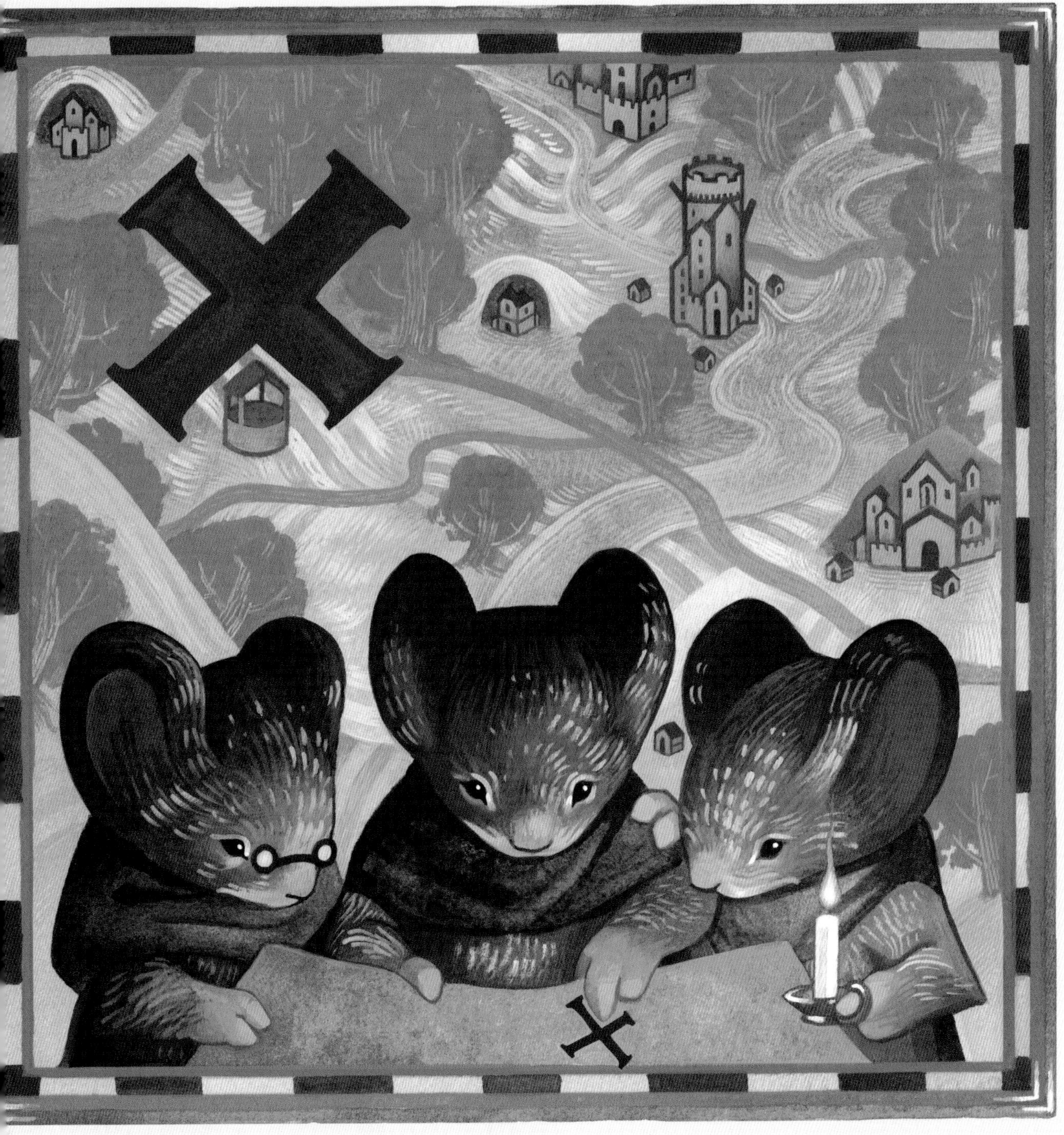

is for
Yulefrost

On the coldest and darkest long winter night,
celebrate together with hot drink and stew.
Cover the pinecones in warm candlelight,
honor all the past mice that we ever knew.

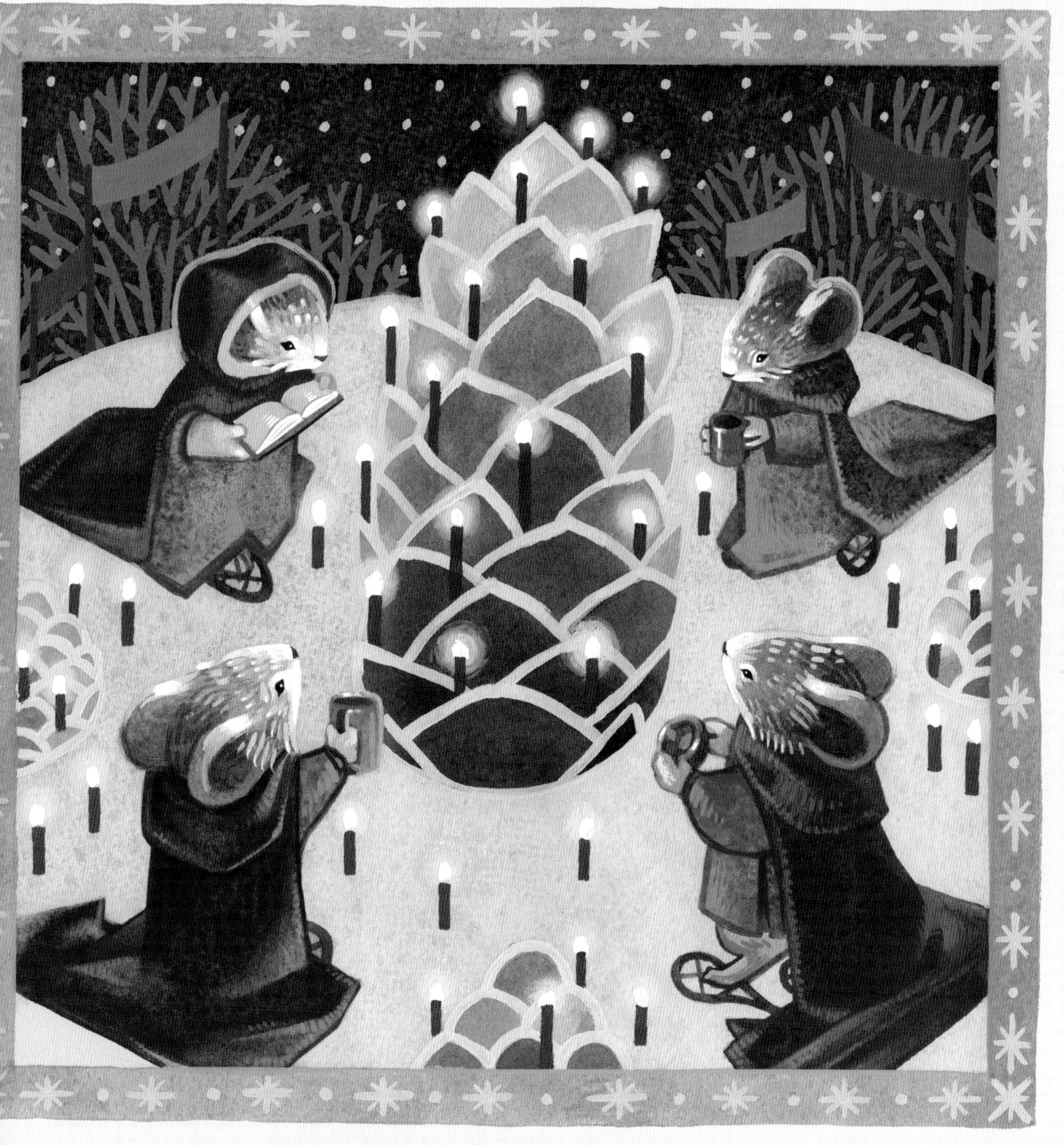

is for
Zephyr

A light gentle wind to push us along,
blows our sails from harbor to shore.
A delicate breeze though not too strong,
so bees can still fly and birds can still soar.

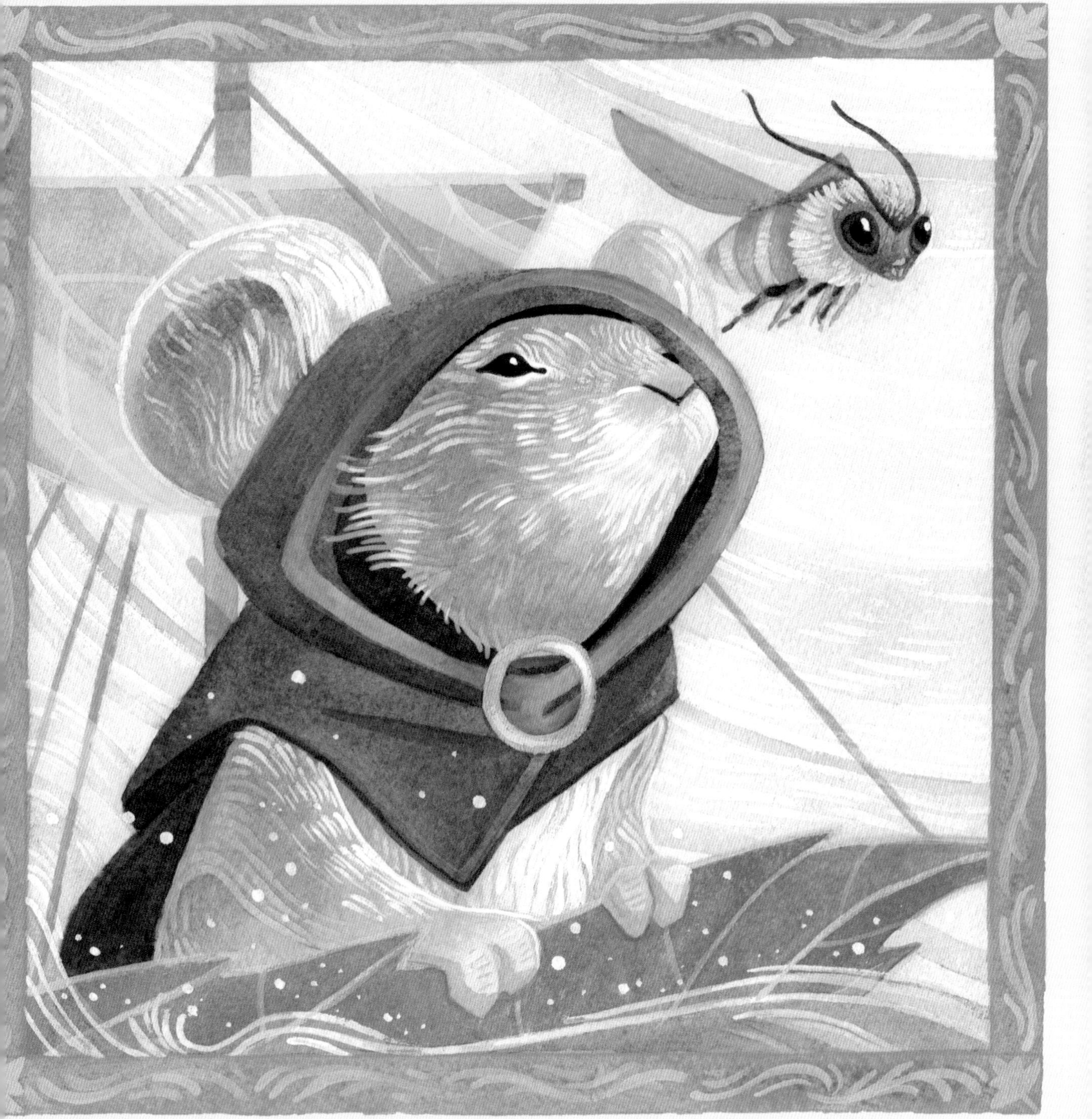

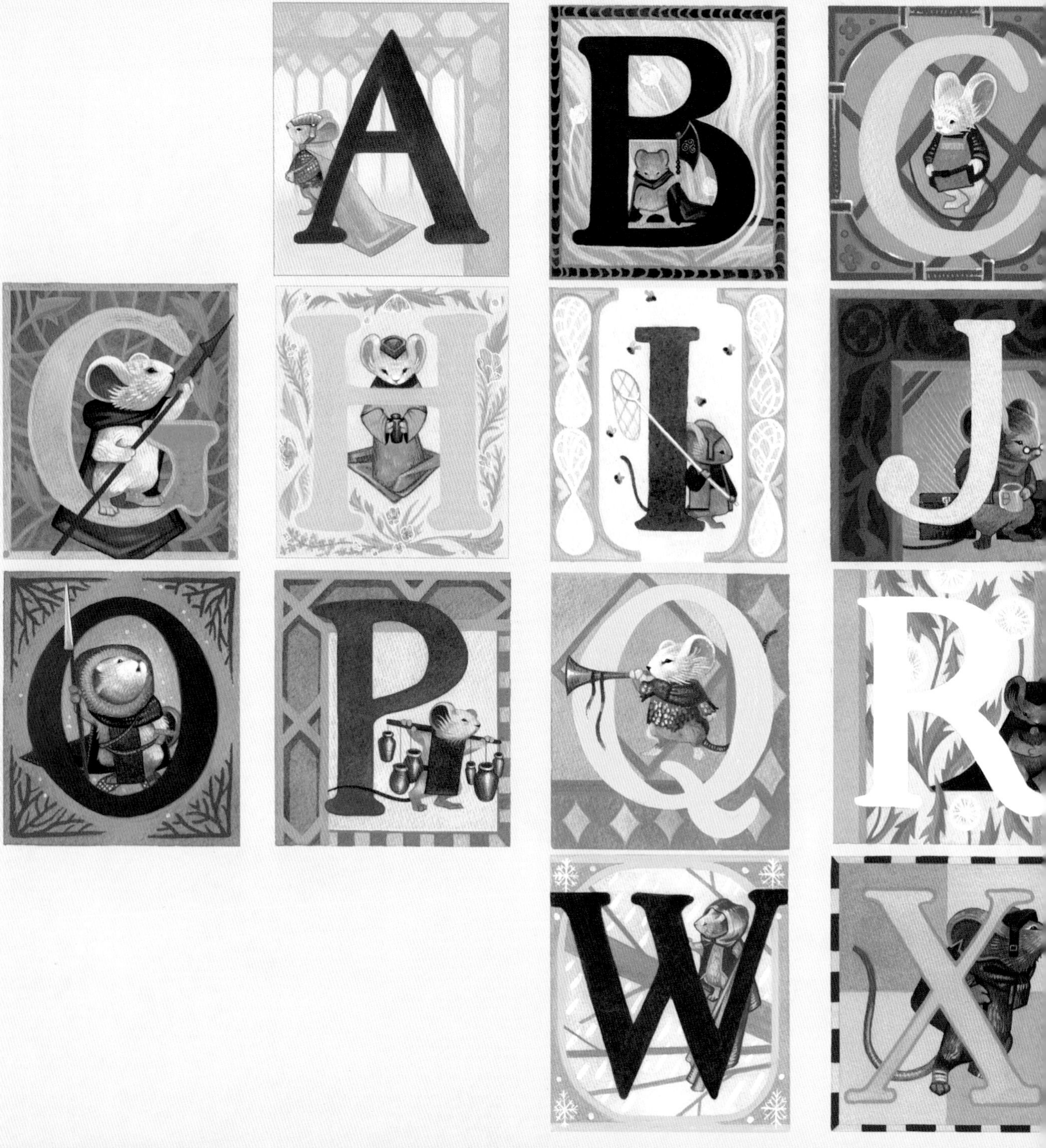
A
B
C
G
H
I
J
O
P
Q
R
W
X

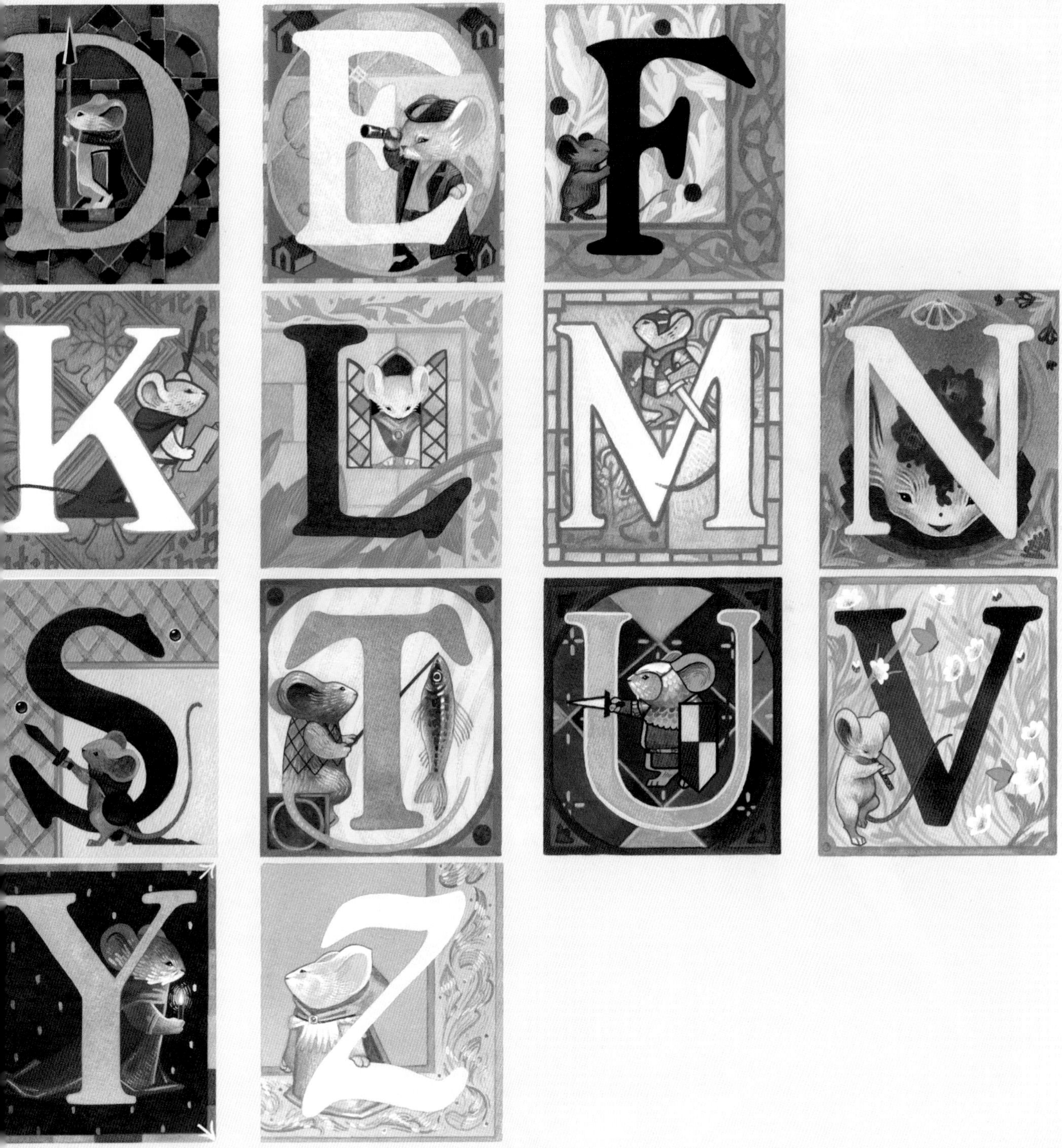
D E F
K L M N
S T U V
Y Z

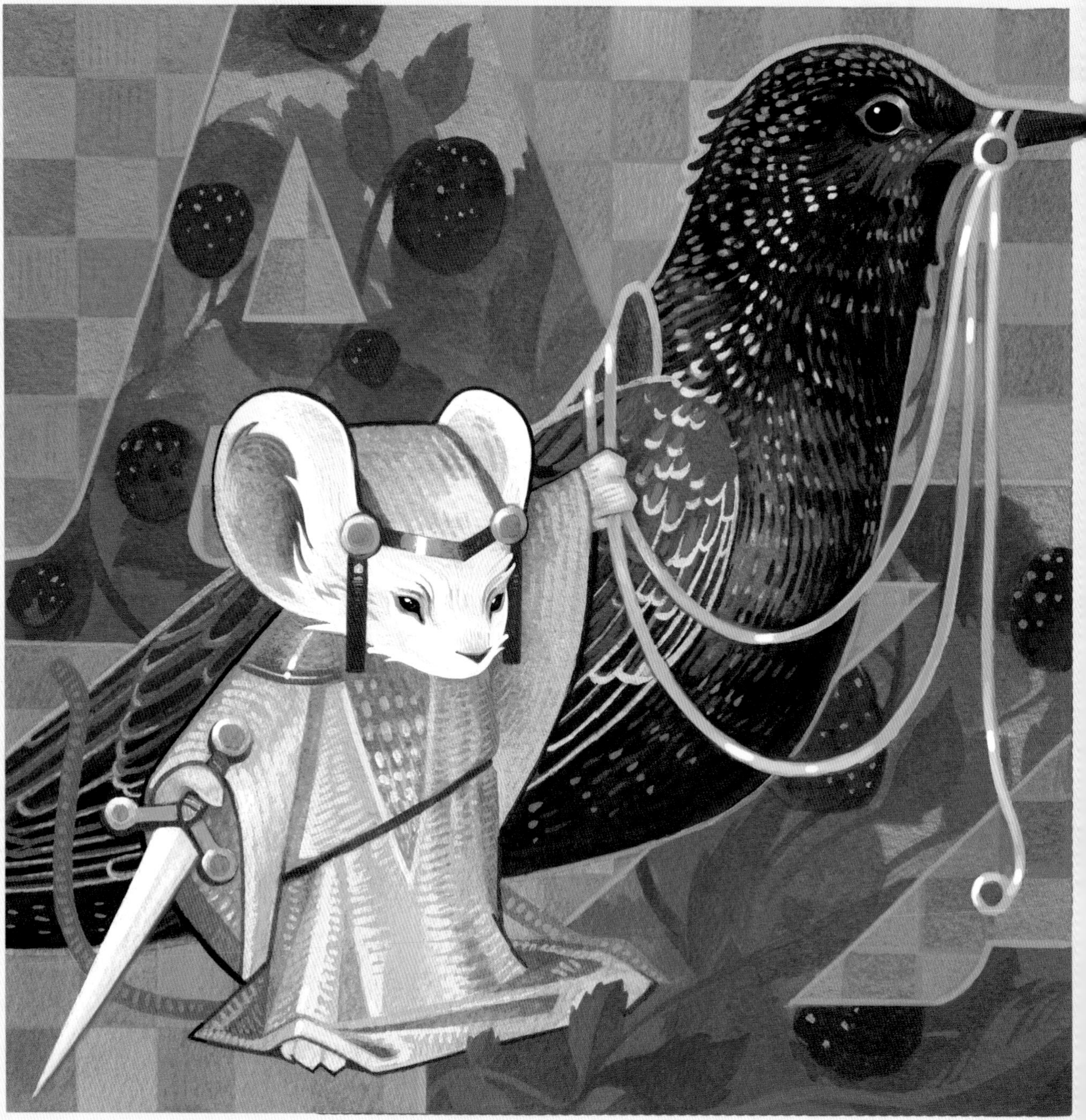

Mice, you must learn these letters well,
all twenty-six symbols, A to Z.
Use them to write and think and spell,
for the tool of language sets ideas free.

Take heed of the lessons I've shared,
mice young, old, or any age between.
You're a bit wiser for these moments spared,
to know your world revealed and unseen.

For so small are we who ride on bird,
wield the sword and harvest grain.
We must be armed with the written word,
as we cross wood and rock, sea and plain.

Serena Malyon was born in 1990. She spent her childhood drawing medieval knights and maidens. In 2012 she graduated from the Alberta College of Art and Design and has built a career on her love of fantasy and adventure. She currently resides in Alberta, Canada, where her hobbies include raising her two cats, playing RPGs, and taking long walks in beautiful places.

David Petersen was born in 1977. His artistic career soon followed. A steady diet of cartoons, comics, and tree climbing fed his imagination and is what still inspires his work today. He is a three time Eisner Award winner and recipient of two Harvey Awards for his continued work on the *Mouse Guard* series. David received his BFA in printmaking from Eastern Michigan University where he met his wife Julia. They continue to reside in Michigan with their dogs Bronwyn & Coco.